THE MYTHOLOGY OF CYPRUS

ACKNOWLEDGEMENTS.

I wish to thank the poet George Szirtes who edited and made valuable additions to the chapter "The Travels of Bronteas". Also to Tina Brown and Margaret Paraskos who helped me do the illustrations.

I SBN: 978-0-9929247-7-5

THE MYTHOLOGY OF CYPRUS

Originally published by Pefkios Georgiades Publications, Nicosia, Cyprus.

This facsimile edition of the 1981 publication, published 2016 by
the Orage Press, 16A Heaton Road, Mitcham, Surrey, CR4 2BU, England.

CONTENTS

Introduction
by Michael Paraskos

There is a nice story told by David Haste, who was Stass Paraskos's former boss at Canterbury College of Art (now the University for Creative Arts) in southern England.

In the early 1980s, when the British government was encouraging the independent art schools to merge with the universities, there was a meeting held at Canterbury to discuss what research meant in a university. Of course, in those days it meant, almost exclusively, publishing a book. So David asked his staff at the meeting to put up their hands if any of them had ever written a book. At first, he says, no hands rose. That was not surprising as terms like research were rarely used in art schools. Art schools were staffed by artists, and what they did was called practice, not research, and it meant doing things like painting paintings and sculpting sculptures, but almost never writing books. Nonetheless, eventually, a single hand rose into the air. One person on the staff had written a book, and that person was Stass Paraskos, a painter and occasional sculptor. And the book he had written was called *The Mythology of Cyprus*.

In many ways, Stass's book was a surprise. Although he was a prolific reader, Stass was never a natural academic. In fact he hated the word academic, and like most artists of his generation, he used it as a term of abuse. So to find himself the only member of staff at Canterbury art school who had done anything that approached what a university in the 1980s would call academic research was the source of much amusement to him. This was especially so given his own background. He had been born into a very poor peasant farming family in Cyprus in the 1930s, and arrived in England a penniless immigrant in the 1950s. As a child he had attended school intermittently, but he had no qualifications. Even as an art student in the late 1950s, he was as much outside the education system as part of it. Attending Leeds College of Art, then under the leadership of charismatic teachers such as Harry Thubron, Tom Hudson and Tom Watt, he had to be an unofficial student as he lacked the formal qualifications to become a properly registered member of the college. As a result he never held a DipFA, the precursor to the BA in Fine Art, and he certainly never gained anything like a BA or MA in art. In fact, the only formal qualification he ever received was in 2008, long after he had retired from teaching, when the University of Bolton awarded him an honorary doctorate for his services to art and education.

By 1981 Stass was, of course, very much a fixture in the British art world. so perhaps we should not be surprised he was no longer the peasant boy from Larnaca, but an ambitious artist and art teacher, keen to experiment, not only with his paintings and sculptures, but with writing and publishing. There is some evidence for this sense of creative ambition. In 1968 he had the almost crazy idea of establishing the first art school in Cyprus, enlisting the support of President Archbishop Makarios to do so. The following year the precursor to what became the Cyprus College of Art, the Cyprus Summer School, was duly founded in Famagusta, with Stass and a dozen British art students mainly from Leeds, spending the summer months in the city. Growing out of this Stass and the Cyprus Artists' Union EKATE, published a magazine of drawings, poetry and stories written by the participants in the Summer School, called *Poseidon*. Many of the elements later found in *The Mythology of Cyprus* can be found in this journal. In 1969 too, Stass published a kind of early book art publication, called *Cyprus of Copper*, which was again a kind of precursor to *The Mythology of Cyprus*. But this only makes Stass's achievements even more remarkable. Stass was born into the poor peasant class in Cyprus, a group still ridiculed as backward by urban Cypriots. But here was a "peasant" teaching in British art schools, starting the first art school in Cyprus and writing books!

If Stass's background made him an unlikely candidate to write a book, then the subject matter of *The Mythology of Cyprus* made it an unlikely book for him, or anyone else, to write. The idea that Cyprus, or at least Greek Cypriots, might have had a distinctive social, cultural or religious history to the Greeks of Greece, was almost unthinkable. Not only did it fall foul of academic snobbery, which even today often discounts ancient, Byzantine and medieval culture on the island as being no more than a degraded and peripheral version of more mainstream cultures, but it went against Greek nationalist narratives that stressed the Greeks of Cyprus should be joined with the Greeks of Greece because they are one and the same people. From a nationalist perspective, any suggestion of a unique Cypriot culture was to fall into the trap once set by the colonial British authorities, and used by them to prevent *enosis,* or the union of Cyprus with Greece. Even as late as the 1980s such attitudes were not uncommon.

From these points of view, the idea of a distinct mythology of Cyprus was a nonsense, as the island's ancient mythology was simply seen by most people as Greek mythology.

It has to be said, I do not think Stass set out to challenge these ideas about historical Cypriot culture directly. Of course he was a proud Cypriot, but he was also a proud Greek, and he was well aware that in many ways Cyprus was a Greek island. But Stass was also a pluralist, and taking a lead from one of his heroes, the British art theorist Herbert Read, he believed it was a kind of stupidity to think human identity could only mean one thing at a time. In other words the ancient mythology of Cyprus was Greek mythology, but at the same time it was a specifically *Cypriot* Greek mythology, as his book would show. In this he had added authority from the religious leaders of the ancient world. As he states in the opening paragraphs of *The Mythology of Cyprus,* the ancient world was liberal in its attitude to religion, and this led inevitably to discrepancies and contradictions in the way its poets retold religious stories. It was such discrepancies that allowed localised versions of stories to develop, reflecting regional differences in places like Cyprus, and the religious authorities of the time were happy to allow these pluralistic cultures to co-exist.

As a consequence *The Mythology of Cyprus* is not simply a book that retells bog-standard Greek mythology (whatever that is) with an idiosyncratic title mentioning Cyprus: it is an oblique plea for the recognition that one can be a Greek and a Cypriot at the same time. Or Turkish and Cypriot, or Armenian and Cypriot, or Maronite and Cypriot, or even British and Cypriot. By the same token someone who is Greek *and* Cypriot does not have to think, act and speak like a Greek from either up or downtown Athens or Thessaloniki. They can be a very different kind of Greek, just as the stories of the Greek gods in *The Mythology of Cyprus* are at times very different to the stories of the Greek gods told in more mainstream texts.

Perhaps I am overplaying the case for an oblique political agenda in this book, but as anyone who knows Stass's art will attest, he was a highly political painter. In his writings too, most of them written in Greek for newspapers in Cyprus, he was deeply committed to the political causes of freedom, human rights and straightforward human decency. I believe this political agenda is present throughout the book.

Although Stass inevitably drew information on the Greek gods from well-known ancient Greek sources, including Homer and Hesiod, he made great play as to how these gods were worshipped specifically on Cyprus. Particularly notable is his description of the worship of Aphrodite at the Temple of Aphrodite, near what is now called Kouklia. Notable too is the way he devotes a whole chapter to the continuing survival of elements of pagan worship into modern times. These survivals, he tells us, are evident within the customs of both the localised Greek Orthodox Church of Cyprus and in Cypriot village traditions, many of which were shared by the Greek, Turkish and other communities on the island. Indeed, it is perhaps this single chapter that stands out most strongly in the book as it was not the product of the extensive reading Stass did for other chapters in the text, but was written after various trips into the Cypriot countryside, often accompanied by a visiting

British artist friend, and talking to villagers themselves. Stass's genius in all this was to marry the latter day customs he discovered with his knowledge of ancient religious practises.

With the dramatic changes in Cypriot life since the book was first published in 1981 it is perhaps unsurprising that so many of these village customs are now lost, making *The Mythology of Cyprus* a curious final record of an older Cypriot way of life prior to the island's assimilation into the modern world.

Yet, perhaps one of the most remarkable features of *The Mythology of Cyprus* is the interjection into what purports to be a non-fiction book of a fictional story, 'The Travels of Broneas'. If anything was designed to highlight Stass's dislike of academic convention it is surely this mixing of fact and fiction, but it is one of the most delightful parts of the book. Imagining himself as Bronteas, a traveller in ancient Cyprus, Stass tries to give his readers an authentic flavour of the ancient world as it would have been experienced first hand, albeit by a slightly innocent traveller. Speaking from a personal point of view, this was an aspect of the book that troubled me very much when it was first published and I was a teenager. The mixing of fact and fiction seemed such an odd thing to do. Paradoxically it is now one of the parts of the book I love most and, with extra irony, it is a method of writing that foreshadows my own working practice as a writer today. I cannot say if this was where I got the idea from, but perhaps it was.

Whatever the case, I think I realise now that what Stass was doing when he wrote *The Mythology of Cyprus*, at the end of a very troubled decade in the history of the island, was deliberately to avoid the approach of both the dry academic and the emotionally-crippled nationalist towards Cypriot history and culture. He was proposing instead a new and creative way of thinking about Cyprus and Cypriotness, drawing on the same approach that underpinned his visual art, as a means to move on from the troubles of the recent past.

Again, I accept I might be over-analysing the political motives behind an enjoyable and delightfully readable book, which will bring pleasure to people who are unfamiliar with the mythology of Greece and Cyprus, and those who are perhaps more familiar with mainstream versions of Greek mythology. Stass loved mythology and folklore, and as a celebrated raconteur, he loved the telling of tales. But still I think, somewhere in the malleability of these stories, their essential pluralism, he saw something profoundly human and humane. He saw the right of individuals to revisit and retell stories, each in their own way, to reflect their own time and circumstances.

Michael Paraskos is the son of Stass Paraskos and a novelist living in London.

STASS PARASKOS
The Mythology of Cyprus

CHAPTER ONE

APHRODITE CYPRIS

THE BIRTH OF APHRODITE

According to the central tradition Paphos was the birthplace of
Aphrodite, though many other cities have at one time or other claimed
this distinction. Cythera, Tyre, and the River Ladon in the Pelloponese
have been credited with this honour.

That such discrepancies should occur, is due chiefly to the prevailing
attitude of the period. In Cyprus for instance where the Greek element
in the population had been dominant from an early stage, a very liberal
manner was quite common, whereby people could speak as they liked
about the deities. They even dared to indulge in battles of wits against
them, believing that it was possible to gain their favours by promises,
bribery or flattery. Each man was free to interpret matters in his own
way—there was very little of the religious dogma as we understand it.
The nearest equivalent to a sacred text was poetry—the writing of the
poets wherein they could find diverse views and accounts of the key
legends. Thus it was quite possible for various communities to select
passages which would favour their claim to be the home of the goddess.
This also explains the contradictions we find in Aphrodite's character
thoughout classical literature. Some people believed that she was the
daughter of Zeus and others that she was his mistress but this does
not mean, as some writers have claimed, that the same people believed
that she was both the daughter and mistress of Zeus.

Hesiod describes her birth in the following fashion. He tells how
by the agency of Gaea, her son Cronos the Titan escaped the fate of
his brothers and sisters, who, as soon as they were born were confined
to the infernal regions by their father Uranus, the ruler of the skies, and
how, when Cronos grew up, he witnessed his mother and father making
love among the planets, whereupon he mutilated the evil Uranus, cast-
rating him so that his genitals fell into the sea.

1

The severed organs floated for a long time in the ocean and a white foam gathered round them, which was fertilized by the sperm. Out of this strange froth sprang a beautiful goddess. At first the winds carried her towards Cythera but then Zephyrus, the west wind, took command and guided her to the Cyprian coast, to the site of Paphos, where she was welcomed by the Seasons and by Eros, the winged god of love, who was to be her constant companion. Wherever her feet touched the ground there blossomed all manner of flowering plants. The Graces then dressed her in the kind of attire that they themselves assumed when attending the dances of the immortals, decking her luxurious gowns and jewels, and setting a crown of gold upon her head. Accompanied by Eros and Pothos, the god of longing, she journeyed thence to Olympus in order to claim her place among the assembly of gods. Here she was named Aphrodite because she was born of the sea-foam, and Cypris as Cyprus was the land where she first appeared. Her great beauty aroused the envy of the goddesses, but the gods greeted her with enthusiasm and many tried to gain her affection.

The father of gods, Zeus, allocated her a very wide realm. She was to be the goddess of beauty, the queen of all aspects of love, the guardian of young girls, and governess of the fertility of animals and plants, (to this end a number of prolific creatures were to be her sacred symbols including the goat, the rabbit, the sparrow, the rosebush, the myrtle and the apple tree whose consecrated fruit used to be given by priests to women who wished to become pregnant). In addition she was to be the protectress of women in dangerous vocations such as prostitutes who were allowed to exercise their profession in some of her temples; and the guardian of marriage in which office she was offered sacrifices at wedding ceremonies. Widows and spinsters prayed to her for a partner.

The cult of Aphrodite spread to all the Mediterranean countries resulting in the multifarious nature of the Aphrodite we know. Her surname varied according to the place of worship; thus at Paphos, she was known as Aphrodite Paphia but other cities refered to her by their own respective titles, of Amathusia, Cythera, Exopolis, Collias Etc. Besides her toponimic titles, there were also surnames that were derived from the natures of various cults. For instance in some places she was called Epistrophia because of her association with incestuous enjoyment; elsewhere she was known as Philomeda for her love of the phallus, Philomeis for her love of laughter, Hetera for her patronage of prostitutes, Apaturia because she deceived in love, and Verticordia because she made women cultivate chastity. At Thebes she was worshipped under three

2

separate names. It is not surprising therefore that Aphrodite has been thought to be the common name for several goddesses, for even her lineage was disputed, some believing her to be the daughter of Uranus, while others affirmed that Zeus and Dione were her parents.

Her two most common surnames were Urania (which means heavenly) and Pandemos (universal). Many people believed that under the first she was the goddess of spiritual love and under the second of sexual pleasures but this is dubious for some temples, such as those of Corinth and Paphos, while being dedicated to Aphrodite Urania were in fact notorious centres of sexual activity. That many people believed her to be promiscuous is due to some extent to her connection with fertility, but to give an example of the contradictory nature of the legends surrounding her, the following story tells of her as the protectress of young virgins.

Pandareus had stolen the golden dog that watched over the temple of Zeus in Crete. He gave it to Tantalus, the king of Lydia, who when confronted by Hermes, denied possession of the article and thus incurred the wrath of the gods. Hermes, who was not deceived by the king's talk, seized the golden dog by force and dumped Mount Sipylus on top of the impious monarch. The thief Pandareus, who had fled to Sicily, perished soon afterwards along with his wife leaving two young daughters

3

called Merope and Cleodora, who would not have survived for long, had not Aphrodite taken them into her care. She fed them with milk and honey and wine, and cultivated their exceptional beauty, persuading the other goddesses to be liberal with their gifts, so that wisdom, joy and skill made them into models of ideal womanhood. When the girls matured, Aphrodite went to Olympus, to ask Zeus for kind and tender husbands for them, but in her absense the cruel Harpies carried off the virgins and gave them as slaves to the Erinyes, the avenging deities, as punishment for their father's crime.

This story illustrates Aphrodite's love of innocence and there were many cases where, in spite of the generally held opinion that her temples were centres of licentiousness, strict rules of chastity were imposed on the priestesses. In the temple of Aphrodite Akrea in Cyprus, for instance, where Aphrodite was represented holding a flower in one hand and an apple in the other, only virgins were accepted for the priesthood. Her more scandalous reputation was got chiefly in times of moral decadence, like the Hellenistic period when the queens of Ptolemaic Egypt claimed to be personifications of the goddess in her role as the queen of love and their courts built altars and temples to them, and the nobles organised orgiastic feasts for their mistresses, all of whom were named after Aphrodite.

APHRODITE'S HUSBAND

Although Aphrodite was worshipped as the guardian of married life, she herself was not a faithful wife. This may have been due to her misfortune in being paired with Hephaistus, a match to which she did not willingly assent, but appearances apart her husband was not an unattractive character. He was the god of fire and the patron of all those who worked in metal; he was the greatest of all craftsmen and came of the highest stock being the child of Zeus and Hera. But at his birth he was found to be lame and so ugly that his disgusted mother cast him from the heights of Mount Olympus into the ocean in the hope that he would be drowned. However he was fated to be saved by the sea-nymphs Thetis and Eurynome who carried him to the ocean bed where they looked after him for nine years.

He was so grateful for their kindness that he made for them several artifices in metal. Finding that he had an aptitude for this he practised assiduously until he became a supreme craftsman, so skilled that he was

4

able to make two ingenious statues that were able to walk and act as his assistants.

Hephaistus then set about wreaking revenge on his mother. He constructed a splendid throne of gold fitted with secret chains and sent it to Hera, who was so thrilled with it that she immediately sat down, touching off the cunning mechanism. At once the chains held her fast and she was powerless to remove them. Neither were the other gods any more successful and Hera besides being uncomfortable, felt extremely humiliated. When it was realised that Hephaistus was the only god with ability to release her, the gods sent messengers down to the ocean to plead his assistance, but they met with a blank refusal. Threats and entreaties were of no avail until Dionysus, the God of wine, tricked him into sampling some of his most potent wines, and dumping the intoxicated Smith-god on the back of a mule, transported him to the top of Mount Olympus. Even in his drunken state however Hephaistus refused to free his mother and would only relent when finally the gods promised him the pick of the goddesses for his wife. Being an artist, with a love of beauty he naturally chose the most beautiful of them all, Aphrodite, and thus it was that this most unlikely match was made.

Hephaistus later forgave his mother and thenceforth treated her with respect and on one occasion went so far as to take her part in an argument she had with Zeus. The king of Gods was so enraged by this that in a fit of fury he seized his son by the leg and threw him down from Mount Olympus. This great fall lasted for nine days from top till bottom and that would have been the end of Hephaistus had not the inhabitants of Lemnos caught him just before he reached the ground. The god was grateful to the people of Lemnos and grew so fond of them that he decided to make his home on their island. In his forge he had the assistance of the one-eyed giants named Cyclopes who helped him to make all those wonders of art and craftmanship for which he was famous. His achievements included the construction of the thunderbolts of Zeus, the armour of gods and heroes, the fire-breathing bulls of the king of Colchis and all the palaces of the immortals. His own palace on Olympus was imperishable and as bright as the stars; it contained his own workshop with the anvil and twenty belows. In spite of his skill and labour, Hephaistus was constantly ridiculed by the other gods for his ugliness. Homer describes how this kindliest of gods was mocked as he hobbled round, serving the other gods at banquets on Olympus. Even Aphrodite, his wife mimicked his lameness when she wanted to amuse her lovers.

But Hephaistus was no more faithful to Aphrodite than she was to him, numbering among his mistresses the graces Charis and Aglaia who acted as hand maids to his wife and were responsible for Refinement and Gentleness. None of Aphrodite's children was fathered by him but he had several illegitimate children of his own and he treated them all—both Aphrodite's and his own with kindness and consideration.

On one occasion he managed to turn the tables on his flighty wife and her current lover Ares, the god of War. Ares was one of the twelve Olympians and as such was honoured by the people of Cyprus, though it must be said that this was due more to fear than affection for he was known to be bad-tempered and on occassion extremely brutal. Being the son of Zeus and Hera he naturally inherited their qualities of courage and leadership but Zeus often had to reprimand him for his hot-blooded excesses, which annoyed the other gods. Besides he was impulsive and lack of thought sometimes led to his downfall as when he was defeated and bound by Poseidon's two gigantic sons, Oeus and Ephialtes. This cost him thirteen months of liberty. Another time he challenged Hercules to single combat, in order to avenge the death of his son Cycnus, but was wounded and forced to flee, groaning, to Olympus. Indeed this incident might have cost him dearer had not Zeus intervened in the first place to save him from further punishment. During the Trojan war he tried to play off both ends against the middle by sometimes supporting the Greeks and sometimes the Trojans so that the war was prolonged for ten years. But he did not escape scot free for when a battle was in progress he ventured to attack Athena who knocked him down with a stone. Further evidence of his vindictive nature may be found in the story of Adonis.

Ares had been secretly meeting Aphrodite for some time believing that the arrangements were fool proof but one day as the sun was passing the windows of Hephaistus's palace he saw them entwined on the bed. Hephaistus was at work at the time but the sun, as soon as his course had taken him to a position above the forge, told the smith-god of what he had seen. Hephaistus let out a deep earth shaking moan and wept. In a jealous rage he plotted his revenge. He used all his skill to make from fire and steel a net so strong that it could not be broken, but at the same time so fine that not even a god could see it. When he returned that night he set this net above Aphrodite's bed so that the slightest movement would cause it to drop. Then he announced his intention of paying a visit to the people of Lemnos. The next morning he set off.

On hearing this Ares was overjoyed and threw caution to the winds.

6

He sped to the palace where he met the waiting Aphrodite and straightaway they tumbled onto the bed in a passionate embrace. At this point the net fell on top of them and they were trapped.

Again it was the sun who performed the messenger's role and Hephaistus soon learned of the success of his scheme. He returned home as quickly as he could to find the lovers locked together in the very position that they had first assumed before the net had fallen. The sight of his unfaithful wife arrested in the act of love stung him deeply and in a mixture of exasparation and triumph he uttered a terrible cry which roused the other gods and brought them running to the scene. A delicate situation awaited them and the goddesses blushed and returned to their homes but the gods remained in the hall, nudging each other and laughing heartily at what they saw. Some professed to be outraged but could scarce suppress a giggle, some exchanged well worn truisms applicable to the situation, while Hermes who himself was in love with Aphrodite declared that though all the world watched and the chains twice as constricting he would at once change places with Ares. The other gods continued guying the lovers and some remembered how in such situations it was customary to exact a fine from the adulterous couple.

In the uproar only Poseidon was concerned for the lover's dignity and he urged Hephaistus to let them go, offering to ensure that Ares

would pay the adultery fine. But Hephaistus would have none of it and replied that it was manifestly wrong to stand bail for scoundrels who would seize the next opportunity to escape from their obligations. Only when Poseidon offered to pay the money himself did the cuckolded husband relent and loosen the net.

The embarassed lovers got to their feet and departed rather ungracefully for their limbs were stiff and their muscles cramped from their long entrapment. Ares slunk off to nurse his wounded pride in Thrace while Aphrodite returned to her birthplace where the three Graces bathed her and anointed her with oils and a rare perfume the aroma of which, it was said, never fades. They robed her in rich gowns and soon she was restored to all her radiance and beauty, not yet aware that she was carrying the child who was to be called Harmonia.

But Aphrodite did not forgive the busybody sun who betrayed her to Hephaistus. She avenged herself by inspiring in him a burning passion for Leucothea, daughter of the king of Babylon. In order to introduce himself to Leucothea he took on the appearance of her mother and visited her, but Leucothea's jealous sister, who also loved the sun, discovered what was going on and betrayed them to her father. The king was furious and ordered his own daughter to be buried alive. The sun, unable to save his beloved from death, sprinkled nectar and ambrosia on the tomb and the body of Leucothea was turned into an aromatic shrub.

After the incident which made him the laughing stock of Olympus, Ares transfered his affection to Eos, the 'rosy-fingered dawn'. Aphrodite grew jealous and tempted Eos to numerous love affairs with mortals the last of these being Tithonus, a prince of Troy, by whom she had two sons. Wishing to be bound to her new lover for eternity Eos begged Zeus to make him immortal, but unfortunately she had forgotten to ask for perpetual youth and beauty and soon he grew into a decrepit old man. Eventually he was reduced to a wrinkled mass of flesh, unable to enjoy life in any way and begged the gods to remove him from this world. But he was immortal and his request could not be granted so the gods changed him into a grasshopper instead.

THE CHILDREN OF APHRODITE

At this point we should mention the children born to Aphrodite by her several lovers, for as we have seen she was not a faithful wife.

The child fathered by Dionysus was probably the most notable of these. He was named Priapus and came to occupy quite an important place among the minor gods, indeed in some parts of Italy and Greece, he was worshipped in the same temples as were his mother and father. In Asia Minor he claimed the status of a major god for there he had his own temples and festivals. It is well known that Priapus was of a somewhat peculiar appearance, and the cause of his disfigurement is worth recounting.

Relations between Aphrodite and Zeus' wife, Hera, had never been too happy, for Hera had felt right from the beginning that the young goddess had upstaged her with her beauty.

Besides, Hera had born Hephaistus, a son both lame and ugly and she could well imagine how comely a child of Aphrodite's might be. So she spitefully decided to interfere with the natural process of birth in order to forestall further shame. Feigning friendship with the goddess she offered to assist her at the childs' delivery but her objective was to exercise some power over the new being. Through her interference the child was born deformed in all his parts, he had a human enough face, but the overall shape of the head was that of a phallus and his ears were goatlike. He was in fact the visual epitomy of lust, a subtle caricature of his mother's propensities. Aphrodite was disgusted and so ashamed of his ugliness that she straightway exposed him on a mountain in the hope that he would die. But, as so often happens with things that we wish to lose or destroy, the despised Priapus was found by some shepherds from Lampascus and saved from his intended doom. The appearance of the child was deemed a marvel in the local villages and soon he became the favourite god of the district. Later however they discovered the correspondence between his features and his nature and were forced to expel him owing to the frequency with which he was seducing their wives. As it happened the town was smitten soon after by a terrible disease whose cause they attributed to their dismissal of the strange little god, and so Priapus was reinstated and a great temple was built in his honour which was to become notorious for the riotous denauchery that took place within. Roman brides in later times were required to sit astride an image of Priapus and at Greek marriages an effigy in the shape of the phallus god was carried in procession in a basket. Red priapic amulets were exhibited near prized possessions and were worn by people round their necks for protection against the evil eye. This was because the ancients believe that the gods obscene shape attracted the first and most dangerous glance of a malevolent being. Thus it was a standard practice to place such images in prominent positions near private dwellings and many household goods were given phallic form. In Roman times a stone pillar with a bearded head and errect penis stood outside most public buildings. The customary sacrifice offered to Priapus was an ass because this animal by its braying had woken the nymth Lotis when the god was about to rape her.

Another son of Aphrodite, although the product of a purely divine union attained rather less prominence. Hermes was his father and he was appropriately called Hermaphroditus. Though he was an extremely handsome youth he proved to be of an androgynous nature. But this was not so from the beginning. Ovid tells the story of his transformation.

He relates how at the age of fifteen the boy set out on a long journey in order to acquire knowledge, to encounter and overcome hardship and thus to gain respect and attain manhood. On his way he passed by a fountain of the naiad Samalcis who scorned hunting and all the common pursuits of other nymphs, and who had somehow managed to avoid the notice of Diana the Great Huntress. She was extremely strong willed and rather vain, and when she saw the handsome youth she was determined to make him her own. At first she tried to gain his affection by direct physical advances, but the boy was innocent and merely confused by her behaviour. So she pretended to go away but instead hid herself behind a tree. It being a hot day the boy was tired and thirsty and the cool waters of the fountain were a great temptation. Thinking that he was in absolute privacy he took off his clothes and entered the water, whereupon Samalcis, grateful for this opportunity emerged from her hiding place and was quickly beside him. She attemped by quick movements to twine herself around him but this was not easy as he struggled against her and kept slipping out of her cluthces, they fought a long time, rising and falling from the water but his strength was greater that hers and eventually she began to weaken. Realising that she might lose him she prayed to the gods that they should not be separated, and thus it was that their bodies were there and then joined together and it became impossible to tell whether the new creature was male or female or both. Thenceforth all men who bathed in the fountain of Samalcis became effeminate.

There were two other children sired by gods. They were Eryx fathered by Poseidon, and Harmonia who had Ares for father. Eryx is chiefly known for his foolish challenge to Hercules to a trial of strength, this not surprisingly resulted in his death. He was buried on a mountain in Sicily which thenceforth bore his name.

10

But Harmonia grew up to marry Cadmus, king of Thebes. Everyone attended the marriage ceremony, except Hera whose grudge against
Aphrodite now extended to her children. Of course there were magnificent presents from all the guests but none more beautiful that the necklace
given by Cadmus himself to his bride. It had been made by Hephaistus
whose skill at such crafts was legendary, and it glittered and sparkled as
the light danced on it. Wearing it Harmonia looked more captivating
than ever.

The royal couple lived happily together for some years while Harmonia bore the king five children, a son and four daughters. But it was
on these children that Hera vent her spite, and tragedy and humiliation befell every one of them in turn until the load of grief grew too
heavy for the royal couple to bear and they in their old age abandoned
themselves to self-exile in Illyria, but this only intensified their sorrow

and at last they begged Zeus to relieve them. He heard and acted promptly on their behalf. Cadmus and Harmonia were transformed into serpents winding and coiling around each other; and so that they should be happier in their strange new life, Zeus led them to the blessed fields of Elysium, the resting place for all virtuous heroes.

As for the splendid necklace, it passed through several hands from that time on, but it had acquired an aura of evil, a malevolent influence that proved fatal to those who possessed it, including among others Argonaut Amphiarus, his son Alcmaeon and the king Phegeus. It is said that the last owner of the neoklace offered it in sacrifice in the temple of Adonis and Aphrodite at Amathus in Cyprus.

Aprodite's children, included Aeneas, the hero of the Aeneid, who was conceived during the affair with Anchises. Aeneas was the most illustrious son of Aphrodite by a human father and his story is worth recounting in some detail:

At times the powers of Aphrodite seemed to be quite limitless. It is recorded that even the mighty Zeus succumbed to her enchantments and fell in love with a Phrygian boy called Gannymedes, whom he had carried to Olympus by an eagle to satisfy his desire. Other gods were similarly affected at various times and formed sexual associations with men and women. In consequence Aphrodite became incautious and boasted openly before them of her power. Only the three virgin goddesses were safe from her! Zeus was finally forced to act in order to maintain his authority and turning the tables on her caused her to fall in love with the Trojan prince Anchises.

The love-struck goddess set off for Troy through the clouds, her colourful dress like a haze of fire, shimmering in the air. Arriving at Mount Ida where Anchises was tending his sheep, she was immediately surrounded by wolves, lions, leopards and bears who gazed on her in wonder. She in turn rejoiced in their ferocity and cast desire into their hearts where-upon the creatures withdrew into the shadowed valley and mated with their partners. Anchises was spellbound, and immediately felt the spreading of desire through his body. The involuntary nature of this desire was disturbing but it quickly passed and he saw only the burning beauty of Aphrodite who was herself under a similar spell. It was out of this whirlwind affair that Aeneas, one of the heroes of Troy was born. Poor Anchises however forgot Aphrodite's warning that he should keep their love secret and boasted of it to others, for which sin he was blinded by a thunderbolt from Zeus.

THE FOLLOWERS AND ATTENDANTS OF APHRODITE

Aprodite was attended by several divinites of varying importance among whom were Desire, Persuasion and Fulfilment, who, though representing the qualities signified by their names, had no distinct personalities. Quite different were the three Graces, Euphrosyne, Aglaia and Thalia, who acted as handmaids of the goddess, dressing and anointing her with perfume. These were minor deities in their own right, being the daughters of Zeus and the nymph Thetis, and most Greeks believed them to be perpetual virgins, though in some parts of Greece Aglaia was romantically associated with Aphrodite's husband Hephaistus.

Their domain was over gentleness and refinement being particularly concerned with the fine arts, especially poetry, and sharing many temples with the nine muses, for while the Muses could give inspiration, it required the Graces to give esthetic form to their work. On Olympus when Apollo played his harp, the Graces danced with Aphrodite and the Muses sang. All three Graces were extremely popular both among mortals and immortals.

The deities around Aphrodite, were divided into complementary pairs. Desire would create the sexual appetites that Fulfilment satisfied, and Eros and his brother Anteros formed a partnership wherby the former initiated feelings of love while the latter punished those who were not responsive to such. At times Anteros might even seperate mismatched couples. This interaction of positive and negative forces is representative of the belief of ancient Cypriots that creation begins at the point where opposing elements meet, and explains why the goddess of love married the ugly Hephaistus and became the mistress of violent Ares.

Eros, the winged assistant of the goddess has been represented in art and literature as a young man, a child or even hardly more than a baby. The goat, the hare, the rose and the cockerel were sacred to him and according to Hesiod, he was the son of Chaos and accompanied Aphrodite on her journeys abroad. But in some places he was believed to be the son of Aphrodite herself; others still cast him as her lover. Whichever version is adopted the fact remains that he was the goddess's chief minister. He carried a quiver of golden arrows round his shoulders. which when either a god or a man was wounded by one it had the effect of making him fall in love with the first living thing that he set his eye on. Aphrodite made frequent use of his power.

13

Eros was married to Psyche who only joined Aphrodite's entourage after the initial difficulties we relate below. The story of Eros and Psyche shows the goddess in a melevolent mood.

Although Aphrodite was known and acknowledged by all, to be the fairest of all beings human or divine, she herself was capable of experiencing jealousy on account of other women's beauty. The princess Phyche was an extraordinarily beautiful child, and as she grew and developed people began to say that no mere mortal could be as lovely as she, some even went so far as to raise her temples, worshipping her as an incarnation of Aphrodite. Psyche herself was perfectly innocent and not at all vain nevertheless her fame spread and aroused the envy of the goddess who sent Eros down with instructions to wound her so that she should fall in love with the oldest and ugliest man that could be found. But when Eros arrived that night by the sleeping girl's bedside he was so taken with her beauty, that he leant over to examine her closer and, as he gazed at her, the princess, sensing a strange presence in the room, suddenly opened her eyes. Although she could not see him for the darkness he was so lost in admiration that when she awoke he panicked and accidentally pricked himself with one of his own arrows and so fell in love with her. Now he panicked for he realised that this new turn of affairs would certainly infuriate his mistress and that her fury would be accompanied by some punishment. The only solution he could think of was to abduct the girl secretly in the hope that the goddess would not find out so he carried her far off, wending his way through the night air to a secret palace whose existence was unknown. As an additional precaution he did not disclose his identity to the princess and warned her to make no attempt to find out. From then on he visited her every night in the palace, but left before dawn each time so that she was never able to see his face.

Psyche was terribly happy and would have remained so, had not her two jealous sisters sought out the palace and confronted her. The stories she told them of the great joy only increased their envy and they contemplated how they might bring it to an end. They were fascinated by the thought of an anonymous lover, and decided eventually that this in fact was the very point at which they could cause the greatest mischief. They suggested to her that he might be some dreadful monster, simply biding his time before he murdered her. They had heard of a great serpent, they said, that had wrought much carnage in the local villages, and they advised her to find out as quickly as possible whether this was he. When they left, poor gullible Psyche trembled for her life and forgot the happiness she had enjoyed. That night, when Eros was asleep she got out of bed and shone an oil lamp on his face. Expecting the worst she was completely overcome with relief and adoration, but in her excitement her hand began to shake and a drop of hot oil fell onto the god's shoulders. Eros immediately woke, and stung by his lover's lack of faith, disappeared, as did the room, the palace, and all its contents so that suddenly Psyche found herself alone and cold in a strange and desolate place.

Psyche was distraught and stumbled about in the darkness, running in this direction and that, untill at last she came to a river where in desperation she attempted to end her life. But the god of the river was kind and would not close over her, but carried her instead quite gently to the opposite bank. It seemed to her, that perhaps all was not lost for if the gods were concerned enough to save her, they might yet restore her to her lover. Hopefully she began to search for a temple where she might hear some news of him. But she wandered from place to place in vain for no one had any clue to his identity. After many months she was on the point of losing hope again when she came across a temple dedicated to the goddess Demeter who advised her to seek out a particular shrine of Aphrodite's and there beg for mercy. This she did unaware that Aphrodite had already learnt of her affair with Eros and was bent on revenge. She treated Psyche with contempt and set her a number of impossible tasks to perform.

The first of these was to gather into seperate heaps, the wheat, the barley and the millet that had been mixed together in enormous quantities in the temple stores. What was more she was given only a few hours in which to accomplish this, but as she was to give up in despair, an army of ants, sent by her beloved Eros, came to her assistance and completed the job on time.

Next she was ordered to collect the wool of a flock of golden fleeced sheep. This seemed an easier task. She set about it with a light heart and skipped her way down into the valley where they grazed. But at the foot of the hill she came across a friendly god who warned her that all who tried to clip these wild sheep were killed by them and that rather than attempt to do this she should gather up the wool that the sheep had left on the thorny bushes near their pasture. By following his advice she succeeded at this too.

But now Aphrodite, thinking that Psyche must have had assistance set her something far more difficult. She pretended that she had been concerned for her beauty since the birth of her child and that the only way to recover it completely would be to use a magical ointment known only to Persephone, Queen of the underworld. Psyche must go and ask Persephone for some. Poor girl try hard as she might she could not think of a way to accomplish Aphrodite's orders, for it was well known that only the dead had access to the underworld. Once more at the very edge of despair, help was at hand. She heard the voice of Eros advising her how to gain entrance into the kingdom of the dead and what was more important, how to get out of it again. He warned her not to eat anything she was offered there, not to open the box that Persephone would give her.

So Psyche entered into the dark kingdom and though beset with terrors made her request known to its queen. Many times she was offered titbits to relieve her hunger and drinks to assuage her thirst, but faithfully she refused to touch any of them. Eventually Persephone placed into her hands a little casket containing the secret of beauty, and bade her take it to Aphrodite. Psyche tightly clutching the precious object set off on the tortuous route that would lead her back to her own world but as she was proceeding on her way she fell to thinking about its contents and soon the idea crept to her that perhaps Eros would love her all the more, if she were more beautiful. The desire to open it grew stronger by the minute until it completely overcame her. Finally she could not stop herself. As soon as she raised the lid however, the spirit of sleep that Persephone had hidden in the box to guard her secret escaped and enveloped Psyche in a deep trance, so that she fell down and slept. This would have been the end of the affair, had not Eros out of his great love for her, pleaded with Zeus, that he should be allowed to marry his princess. He was moved by their cause and showed mercy, bestowing immortality on Psyche, making her like one of the gods. Futhermore using threats and promises he persuaded Aphrodite to change her mind and agree to the marriage. Later Eros and Psyche had a daughter whom they named Delight.

Eventually Psyche was completely reconciled with Aphrodite and became one of her companions. Her story illustrates that the soul (Psyche), strengthened by love and purified by experience and suffering is capable of overcoming death.

APHRODITE AND THE TROJAN WAR

The most famous of all Greek stories, and the central theme of the Greek imagination is the Fall of Troy. It is interesting that these events were precipitated by the decision of a man who did not give sufficient consideration to his judgement and by the vanity of three goddesses, one of whom was Aphrodite.

And it is with Aphrodite that we begin at the wedding feast of Peleus, King of Thessaly, and Thetis, a sea nymph. All the gods were invited, all that is except Eris, the goddess of strife, who was bad-tempered and destructive. She was furious at this slight and in order to spoil the feast for the others she threw down into their midst, a golden apple bearing the inscription 'to the fairest'. This lovely apple of solid gold rolled along the floor until it came to rest before Hera, Athena and Aphrodite who happened to be standing to-gether. It was immediately claimed by all three and a great quarrel arose between them. If Zeus had not intervened to part them there would have been a fight. Then they appealed to the decision of the other guests but they, being prudent, foresaw that any choice would leave the judge with two powerful and embittered enemies, so politely excused themselves. The case was taken to Zeus himself who did not relish declaring on such a delicate matter, and ordered the goddesses to submit their dispute to the arbitration of thefairest mortal man who at that time was prince Paris, son of King Priam and Queen Hecuba of Troy. "Go to Mount Ida", he said, "to the son of Priam. He is a man of taste, well qualified to pick the winner".

So the three contestants were escorted by Hermes to Mount Ida where Paris was tending his sheep. Now, although Paris had a reputation for being fair and wise man, all three goddesses attempted to sway his favour by glowing promises of suitable rewards. In short, by bribery. Hera offered wealth and power, Athene wisdom and skill in war, but Aphrodite guessing intuitively at the man's especial weakness, unbuckled her magic girdle by whose means she had poured desire into innumerable hearts, and promised him the fairest mortal in all the world for his wife. Paris hesitated between the three, but there was really little doubt in his mind as to the choice he would make, for while thoughts of fame, power and wisdom were attractive, beauty was immediate, and seductive. He awarded the prize to Aphrodite thereby gaining at one stroke one friend and two deadly enemies. Nor did he suspect that by doing so he was setting into motion a train of events that would lead to tragedy and disaster.

Time passed and the girl failed to appear, so growing impatient Paris equipped a fleet and set out to find her. He was accompanied on this journey by, amongst others, the son of Aphrodite, Aeneas. The great winds bore them to the coast of Greece and up the river Eurotas, to the city of Sparta, where they were hospitably received by king Menelaus and his wife Helen.

Queen Helen, daughter of Zeus and Leda, was the most beautiful woman of her age. When little more than a child, she had been carried off by Theseus, king of Athens, from whom she was rescued by her brothers the demigods Caster and Pollux. She then married Menelaus, King of Sparta, whereupon her other suitors who were still deeply in love with her, vowed to guard her and her husband from any deeds of violence or injustice.

On the tenth day of the Trojans' stay in Sparta, Menelaus received an urgent message that his grandfather had died and that his presence was required at the funeral, so he sailed for Crete, leaving Helen to entertain the visitors.

The following day, the Trojans also decided to leave. Bidding farewell to Helen they set off in the directon of Salamis, but having sailed only a little way dropped anchor and returned under cover of darkness. That night they abducted Helen together with her baby son and carried them off eventually to Troy. Aphrodite was instrumental in this for she had cast a spell on Helen under whose influence she had believed that Paris was in fact her lately departed husband. Peitho, Goddess of Persuasion, and Eros, whose powers are known, were also implicated.

Having achieved his ambition, Paris sailed first to Cranae and spent the night with his newly captive wife. He was hardly able to tear himself away from his beautiful captive. On they sailed towards Troy but the following day a violent storm interrupted their voyage and they were pleased to find shelter in Cyprus, which was rather off their course. Under the circumstances they made for Sidon next, where Paris, still intoxicated by his success, murdered the local king and plundered his treasury to provide presents for Helen. Then once more they set out for Troy and eventually reached home by way of Phoenicia and Egypt. Priam, whose own sister had been carried off to Greece by Hercules and forced to marry Telamon, welcomed this opportunity to pay off old scores and gladly accepted Helen into his household.

In the meantine, Menelaus, having been informed of the recent outrage, made all speed for home, and began to make preparations for a retributive war. His cause was acknowledged to be just and all Greece took arms on his bahalf, his own brother Agamemnon being chosen chief of staff of the combined forces. Agamemnon went round recruiting allies and it was now he attempted to involve Cinyras of Paphos in the war by sending Talthybius, Odysseus and his own brother the aggrieved Menelaus, to Cyprus. Cinyras promised to help but when the Greeks left he sent only one ship as token assistance. To appease the anticipated wrath of the recipient, Cinyras also made a personal gift to Agamemnon, that of a magnificent breastplate, whose description may be found in the 'Iliad'. But the Greeks anyway were too preoccupied with their preparations to consider taking any penal action so Cyprus remained in peace and increased in prosperity.

As for the Greek allies, they gathered at Aulis, in north-eastern Greece where Agamemnon began his campaign by capturing Tenedos, a port guarding the approach to Troy. From here he progressed to Troy itself and sent an embassy, under a flag of truce, to demand the return of Helen. The demand was refused. The Greeks then attacked Troy.

So the war started and it soon became obvious that the two sides were equally matched; battle after battle, sortie after sortie proved inconclusive. Though losses were heavy and the armies found themselves

19

drifting into the second, then the third, then the fourth year and all without any significant progress by either side. The gods too were equally divided on the issue; Hera and Athena abetting the Greek cause while Aphrodite, her lover Ares, and Apollo supported Troy. Others involved were Poseidon, Hephaistus and Hermes on the Greek side and Artemis and Iris of the rainbow, on the Trojans. Zeus remained aloof most of the time but his sympathies lay with the Trojans rather than the Greeks. As for Thetis, though she remained on the fringes of the action, her son Achilles was fighting for Agamemnon so she naturally extended a protective hand to him now and then.

Unhappily, Aphrodite though not without courage was no match for the others in warfare and was twice wounded. Once she was struck by a Greek arrow and had to resort to Olympus and the healing ointments of Dione when Zeus, concerned for her safety, advised her to stick to what she knew, namely the art of love, and leave the fighting to those who were more suited to it. But she had her commitments to Paris and Aeneas, so she ignored his warning and returned to the fray. Though she failed to influence the final outcome of the war she managed to give effective help to individual Trojans at times of mortal danger. The following incident tells of one such occasion.

The war now being in its ninth year, Paris was persuaded by his brother Hector to end it by arranging an individual contest between himself and a volunteer from the other side. So Paris stepped forward and declared that he would meet any Greek in single combat so that the issue might be settled once and for all. Menelaus, glad of this opportunity to avenge his wrongs accepted the challenge at once, but when Paris saw who was to be his opponent, was struck by fear and guilt and tried to slip back into the company, terrified. Then Hector, his brother, the greatest hero of the Trojan forces, heaped abuse on him and shamed him into reassuming his position on the field of combat. All the men cheered this as they were sick and tired of the continual slaughter and lack of results and the agreement was solemised with oaths, wine and the blood of a lamb. Helen herself joined the Trojan king on the city wall to witness the contest, her heart by now being fully on the side of her former husband. Indeed she had grown to despise Paris once the spell had worn off.

The two rivals took up their positions in no-mans land and faced each other with sword and spear. Paris, having won this right by lot, threw his spear first and struck Menelaus' shield but failed to pierce it.

20

Menelaus after a short prayer to Zeus, cast his and broached his oppo-net's spear and breastplate. But Paris twisted and turned his body so that the point only grazed his side. Next, Menelaus drew his sword and struck his enemy powerfully on the helmet ridge, breaking his sword in the process, but knocked Paris over. This was enough to give the king a second's advantage and he leapt on Paris furiously, seized him by the crest of his helmet and began dragging him towards the Greek lines. That would have been the end of Paris had not Aphrodite chosen this time to intervene. Invisible, she stood next to Paris and wrapping him in a dense cloud removed him from view of the spectators and of Menelaus, dropping him some distance behind the Trojan line. The astonished armies concluded that Paris must somehow have fled and were disgusted by such cowardice. Menelaus rightly claimed his victory and his wife and would certainly have been awarded both, but just before a final decision was reached the Trojan Pandarus, being misled by Athene who did not wish Troy to escape the doom her vengeance demanded, fired an arrow at Menelaus and wounded him. This treachery infuriated the Greeks who spontaneously fell upon the Trojans in force, thus robbing Menelaus of his victory.

The day was not yet finished for, urged on by Agamemnon, battalion after battalion of the Greek soldiery swept into battle, forcing Hector and his Trojans to retreat in disarray. Indeed the Trojans suffered the greater losses and the gods flocked from Olympus to add their weight to one side or the other in the crisis. Athene was personally responsible for the death of many Trojans including her unwitting tool, Pandarus, and she also contrived to injure Aeneas who would have perished had not Aphrodite protected him from further harm by rendering him invisible.

But the battle was dominated by one man, the Greek Diomedes. First he attacked Aphrodite and cut her hand at the base of the palm causing her great pain and forcing her to flee the field to the peace of Olympus, though she left Apollo in charge of her son. Next, when Ares burst vengefully on to the scene and wreaked havoc among the Greeks, Diomedes confronted him, chariot to chariot and wounded the god of war severely in the belly, whereupon Ares let out a yell so loud that the mountains trembled. So Ares too was forced to retire from the scene. Of course Diomedes had not achieved this without divine assistance, for it was Athene that had manoeuvred their meeting in the first place, and had diverted Ares' spear from its course so that it landed harmlessly in the dust. Nevertheless Diomedes had already been wounded twice so his actions showed great courage. He was to be a scourge to the Trojans throughout the war and returned safely to Argos, his kingdom. But Aphrodite would not let him off so lightly and in revenge for her injury, stirred up trouble in the land and made his wife unfaithful to him so that at last Diomedes left his home in despair and died in weary exile.

Other men notable on the Greek side were Teucer, Nestor, Odysseus, Aias and of course Achilles, but this last had quarelled with Agamemnon at an early stage of the war about the possession of a captive girl named Briseis, so his decisive contribution was not felt until the last stages of the war.

It was at this time that Paris was wounded and returned to his first love (some say his true wife) Oenone, whom he had abandoned for Helen. She possessed healing powers but having been deeply hurt by his rejection of her, found it impossible to forgive him and withheld her aid so that Paris grew weak and finally died. But Oenone was unable to live on after his death for she had loved him very deeply, and shortly afterwards she hanged herself in a fit of remorse. On Paris' death, his brother Deiphobus claimed Helen's hand as of right and forced her to marry him, but this was not to be a lasting state of affairs, for that cunning artifice, the wooden horse was already in construction behind the Greek lines.

This had been the idea of one Calchas who was an inspired prophet. His plan was to build a gigantic wooden horse whose middle would be hollowed out so as to accommodate a large number of fighting men. The horse itself was to be constructed by Epeius with the help of Athene.

When the horse was complete the Greeks chose their finest warriors to man it, they burned their wooden huts and sailed for Tenedos. The battle ground was left deserted save for the horse. The Trojans were suspicious at first and standing round it debated what to do. Some said they should burn it, others wanted to hurl it from the rocks, but in the end they all agreed to dedicate it to Athene. Then they turned to mirth and feasting believing the war to be over. Apollo's priest, Laocoon, warned his Trojan countrymen not to trust the Greeks, and struck his speat into the side of the horse but before he could convince them, two enormous serpents rose from the sea advancing at great speed, and killed Laocoon together with his two sons. The Trojans convinced that the serpents had been sent by Athene to punish the priest tried to make amends by dragging the ill-omened horse into their city demolishing part of the city wall in the process. Aphrodite, aware of the danger made one last attempt to save Troy. She cast another spell on Helen, who had been informed of the Greek plot, and made her betray the secret to Deiphobus. But he did not believe her and that very night the Greeks emerged from their horse and opened the city gates.

Aphrodite's spell this time lasted only an hour and when it wore off, Helen sat at the window of her bedroom and gave the signal for the newly returned Greeks to attack, whereupon Troy was inundated by hostile troops, and the population including Deiphobus and Priam, massacred. Very few Trojans survived the ensuing bloodbath. Cassandra, who had been prophesying the destruction of Troy ever since Paris had returned from Greece, was taken prisoner and was to be murdered in Sparta. Queen Hecuba all of whose children had perished was soon to meet a tragic end, being changed into a wolf. Andromache, Hector's faithful wife was sold into slavery and her children slain. Aeneas managed to escape after valiant resistance. Before he left the burning city he spotted Helen, alone, in the porch of Hestia's temple. Enraged that the cause of so much suffering should still be living among the general slaughter he determined to kill her, but his mother Aphrodite suddenly appeared and bade him look after his own family who were in mortal danger. "The destruction of Troy was not caused by Helen", she said to him. "But by the avenging gods". Aeneas managed to save his son Asconius and his blind father Anchises whom he carried on his shoulders, but his wife Creusa was lost in the darkness and he could not find her. The family sheltered for a while on Mount Ida and Ascanius returned to Troy to help a band of refugees. As for Aeneas after many adventures which took him to Delos, Crete, Carthage and Epirus he arrived in Italy where he married Lavinis daughter of king Latinus, and settled in Lavinium, Rome's forerunner. The Trojans and Latins adopted each others customs, laws and religion and were united under the single name of the Latins. But Aeneas did not live long to enjoy his new realm. He died in battle and Aphrodite persuaded Zeus to admit him to the rank of the gods. Aeneas's father Anchises had died soon after their arrival in Italy and lay buried in Aphrodite's temple on Mount Eryx in Sicily. The deification of Aeneas set the pattern for the deification of Roman emperors.

Helen was dicovered by Menelaus in her chamber. At first he intended killing her, but catching sight of her breast unveiled, he cast his sword away. So he took her home, though that journey too was not without incident for she was again abducted on the way, her beauty being still a strong temptation to others, and Menlaus had to seek her in Cyprus and Egypt. His arrival in Cyprus co-incided with the death of his old friend and comrade in the wars, Demophon. When Menelaus himself died Helen was driven from Sparta and took refuge in Rhodes with its queen, Polyxo, whom she believed to be her friend. But Polyxo's husband had been killed in Troy and she held Helen responsible so, one day when Helen was bathing, the queen sent two of her servants, dressed as Furies, who seized her and hanged her on a tree.

Agamemnon on his return home was murdered by his treacherous wife Clytemnestra and a tragic blood feud ensued among the members of his family.

Troy after its destruction, remained in ruins for along time. Eventually a new town was founded but it remained a modest place until Roman times. The Romans felt a special responsibility to-wards Troy because they considered themselves as descendants of Aeneas. The leading Roman families claimed direct descent from Aphrodite herself, and for this reason, when Troy became part of the Roman Empire it was accorded special privileges and was treated as an independent state. The new Trojans were granted extensive territories and exception from paying taxes, as a consequence of which their town grew and prospered; at the same time their old enemies, the Greeks, were occupied by the Romans and most of the cities that joined Agamemnon in his expedition against them lay in ruins or were reduced to insignificant villages.

CHAPTER TWO

MYTHOLOGY OF CYPRUS : THE CINYRAID CYCLE

PYGMALION AND GALATEA

When Pygmalion was still a young man an incident occured that was to embitter his consequent outlook and turn him into a hater of women. At that time the law of his native city Amathus, dictated that all women should sleep with a stranger before their marriage because it was believed that if a husband happened to be the first lover of his wife he would rival the gods in her affections. However the daughters of Amathus saw fit to defy the law, wishing to remain virgins right up to their wedding so in order to punish them, the goddess Aphrodite planted in them an insatiable sexual appetite which caused them to lose all shame and offer themselves to all men indiscriminately. The citizens were bewildered and the women themselves suffered a variety of pains and discomforts as a result: they sweated, they itched, they were unable to sleep, they became irritable and scolded their husbands and children on any petty excuse: in fact they became downright unbearable both to others and to themselves, so that in the end some of them began to long for death as a relief. Some took to wandering in the streets at night half naked in the hope of attracting lovers, others roamed the woods and fields and resorted to venting their lust on harmless animals; it was very degrading. But their punishment was not yet complete, for Aphrodite, some say from motives of vengeance, some say pity, finally turned them into rocks and piled them high at the foot of a hill where they may still be seen. They go under the name of The Propodides.

Pygmalion was so disgusted with the women's behaviour that he decided to shun all female company and dedicate himself entirely to his work. He spent the days and nights in the silence of his studio, carving figures out of wood and marble, gradually improving his technique until his creations became so lifelike that they might have been mistaken for living men and women. But satisfaction eluded him for he was intent on producing a statue so perfect that it would quite eclipse even his most remarkable works. This intense ambition dominated all his thoughts to the total exclusion of any earthly friendship and brought him by degrees to the verge of insanity.

But Aphrodite, took pity on him and taking the form of a most beautiful girl, she appeared to him in a dream and inspired him with the vision he had longed for. When Pygmalion awoke he recalled his dream and set impatiently to work in the hope of capturing her likeness, taking for his materials the finest white ivory, so smooth and white, that it might well have been taken for flesh, though of a rather unearthly kind. The statue that he carved far outshone anything he had made before; so flawless, so serene was this image, that for hours on end he sat watching it, willing it to move or to speak. Thenceforth each day he would do this, and indeed at times he came to imagine that now her lips parted, now a hair trembled in the draught; sometimes life itself would seem to suffuse her face and then he would stretch out his arms to touch her, but finding her cold he would relapse into his listless admiration. Sometimes he kissed the statue and spoke to it tenderly. He rarely left her side, and when he did it was only to wander alone by the sea or in some distant valley where he could gather flowers, or amber or bright pebbles for her. He dressed her with expensive silks, put rings on her fingers, long necklaces round her neck. Pygmalion then placed the statue on a couch that was covered with cloths of Tyrian purple and called it his bedfellow. As time went on his passion for her grew and so did his melancholy.

Aphrodite was the guardian goddess of Amathus and her festival was celebrated with great pomp. Heifers with gilded horns were prepared for sacrifice, a dozen at a time, and the temples were filled with incense; priests wore their finest ceremonial garments and the laity milled in the gardens and colonnades. On the day of the festival Pygmalion took with him an offering of great value, stood by the altar and prayed fervently that his statue be given life. Aphrodite, seeing his sorrow, was moved to help him. As a sign of her favour, the sacred fire burnt brightly and three times in quick succession a flame leapt into the air.

Gathering flowers from a nearby field he returned home to find a maiden standing where his statue had been. It was most certainly her, his ivory statue come to life. He was quite entranced by her beauty and stood, speechless, not knowing what to do or say; almost automatically he offered her flowers. For a moment she was still, but then she stretched out her arms to accept the bouquet and he touched her skin and found it soft and warm. He wanted to touch her everywhere but she averted her eyes and would not look up at him, neither would she speak. Pygmalion, overcome, muttered a brief prayer of thanks, and taking his courage in both hands confessed his love for her and asked for her hand in marriage. At this a blush rose to the statue's face as she turned again to face him and replied, 'Pygmalion, I know of your love and will indeed be your bride'.

Because of her fair colouring, Pygmalion named her Galatea, which means "the milky one" and soon afterwards he married her. The goddess Aphrodite was present at the marriage. Nine months later Pygmalion's bride gave birth to a daughter, Paphos.

CINYRAS AND MYRRHA

When Paphos grew up she married a Syrian named Sandocus who was then living in Cyprus, but it was in the land of Cilicia that the young couple made their home, and it was there that Paphos conceived and bore a son whom they called Cinyras.

There were legends attached to the birth and early years of this boy: Owing to his great skill on the harp, it was believed that he was in fact an illegitimate son of Apollo, the god of poetry and music. Pindar on the other hand makes him the god's lover. Nevertheless all agree in praising his wisdom, his ingenuity, his athleticism and his comeliness that caused Aphrodite herself to fall in love with him. Many fine qualities and outstanding deeds were attributed to him. The invention of diverse mechanical appliances, the introduction into Cyprus of metals, of weaving, of the potter's craft; and besides all this many miracles and supernatural powers. But setting these aside, the most enduring monument to his memory is the city of Paphos which he himself founded and ruled, and this is how that came about:

Cilicia had been struck by famine: the aged, the infirm, the young and their nursing mothers, these were the first to succumb, but soon the others and something desperate needed to be done. Thus it was that Cinyras and a small band of followers set sail in the hope of discovering some more fertile land and stumbled on the island of Cyprus, on the very coast where Aphrodite herself had been washed ashore in the immemorial past. How pleasant it was here among the fruit and the vines; they were well content to settle in this place. So they built themselves a town, and in the centre of it erected a temple to Aphrodite, who, they believed had guided them to her birthplace, and Cinyras became the first king and high-priest of the new city, which they named Paphos in honour of his mother, and he administered civil and religious laws to his subjects.

Cinyras was neither tyrant not weakling; he set up a council of elders to provide stability and enjoyed a peacable rule. The power vested in the council was considerable; it could, if it wished, veto the throne, appoint the successor, or even in extreme circumstances depose the incumbent. However the executive decisions were left to the king. Cinyras pronounced judgments, declared policies, led the army into war, and, as was his due, claimed the largest share of the spoils. All land owned by the state was available for his use; he had the seat of honour at feasts. All or most of the incidents and customs we shall relate took place while he was king.

Under his rule the temple grew prosperous and Aphrodite showered favours on the city, on the island and indeed on the king himself, making him wealthy and giving him a long reign. By escaping the impoverishing consequences of the Trojan war Paphos became for a while the most powerful state of the mediterranian world. If all this itself could constitue happiness, Cinyras would have been the happiest of men, but his personal life was marred by ill fortune.

His son Amaracos had discovered how to extract the scent off flowers and to make the most delicious perfumes from them. But he hoarded the secret glorying in his ingenuity and before long several of the gods grew jealous of his skill and coveted his delightful store. There was one special amongst them whose envy became an obsession and he finally murdered the young man in a field on the outskirts of Paphos, whereupon his victim was transformed into an herb, that we now call marjoram.

Cinyras was much saddened by the loss of his son but did not allow his grief to interfere with the smooth running of the state. However worse was to come. We have mentioned his extraordinary beauty as a young man, but as he grew older he gained rather than lost in attractiveness, for his features matured with the added dignities of his office and he looked the very image of a god. Unfortunately this aggregation of qualities was not lost upon those nearest to him and in Myrrha his own daughter a dreadful passion arose, far outstripping the normal affection of child to parent. Eventually she found a way to fulfil her craving for him.

Myrrha was a beautiful girl and suitors had gathered from many countries to seek her hand; the princes of Cyprus had come to vie with one another for the privilege of marrying her. Cinyras, faced with such a throng of suitors, did not know what to do and asked Myrrha to make her own choice. She remained silent, gazing at her father though he put this down to girlish modesty. When he asked her what kind of husband

she wanted, she replied 'One like you'. The king was flattered by this and praised her for being so devoted but the fact was that the girl could not choose otherwise. She prayed to the gods in heaven that they should banish her sinful thoughts and extinguish the horrible desire, but none of them responded, not even Eros who denied the accusations of the other gods that it was his bow which had wounded Myrrha. At midnight, when everybody was asleep, Myrrha remained awake consumed by a fire she could not quench. She renewed her prayers and when she saw that there was no response and no end to her despair she decided to kill

29

herself. She tied her girdle to the top of the door-post and fastened the cord around her neck. She was about to Jump to her death from a high stool when the nurse woke up and saved her.

Some time later all the married women of Paphos went out into the fields to celebrate the feast of Demeter the corn goddess, at which they all dressed in snow white garments and offered the goddess garlands made of corn ears, the first of the crop. The king's wife, Metharme, was taking part in the rites which took nine days and during which love making was forbidden. So while the king's bed was empty of its lawful occupant Myrrha determined on her awful course. It was a particularly dark night. The clouds had been building up all day but there was no rain. Instead there was that oppressive closeness hated by those with delicate health, windless and starless. Had Myrrha been more careful of her passion she might have taken these, and other things as omen, instead she stole from her room and padded her way across the courtyard. . . The king lay asleep in his bed and so she came and sat down next to him and caressed his brow gently until he stirred, then like a succubus she seduced him. In the darkness he did not recognize her, furthermore she said nothing so that her voice would not give her away. However she had been clever enough to anoint herself with some stolen perfume, such as the priestesses normally wore, and this was enough to reassure him. She meant to leave then and to wash away her scent, so that she would be unsuspected when the king awoke. But in the heat of the moment she forgot her plans and clung tightly to her father and they fell asleep together. He woke first, recognised his daughter and in his horror and fury drew his sword to kill her. Having awakened to the noise of his rising, she cried out and fled into the palace garden, but being faster he soon caught her up and was on the point of lifting his sword for the fatal blow, when Myrrha, who had fallen to her knees in a desperate prayer, began to change in shape. Her hair became foliage her arms branches and her body began to form a trunk. Soon crisp bark had encased all her parts, and she stood in front of him a blossoming myrtle tree. The king stood transfixed, his upraised sword gleaming in the silver light. Slowly he drew back and as he did so he became aware of Aphrodite sitting amongst the tree's branches, her sparkling gown spread accross the leaves and shoots, her face calm and silvery as the morning itself. "You Cinyras", she addressed him, "stand still and do not harm your daughter. Certainly she has done you wrong but she has been punished. You for your part, for you are not entirely blameless in this, must never damage this tree which is all you have left of her.

No, instead you must build an altar at her feet, and you must worship here daily, for so I command it. And if you do as I say some good may yet come from this matter". This said the goddess disappeared leaving the king and the tree together in the garden.

When Metharme returned there was much sorrow at the fate of Myrrha, and coming so soon after the last tragedy, the loss of Amaracos, it was almost enough to drive them to despair. But their family was large, there still remained to them three sons and six daughters, and as it was, after a long period of mourning they accepted their fate and resigned themselves to the will of the gods.

The goddess's instructions were strictly carried out. Three seasons passed and berries hung in purple clusters from the tree. One day the king was about to burn incense on the altar when the leaves above him trembled and parted and a baby boy of remarkable beauty fell from the branches into his arms. The child grew to be so fair that the Paphians regarded him with religious awe, paying him all sorts of honours and calling him Adonis, which means Lord.

ADONIS

Adonis seemed, even to his contemporaries, to have the nature and appearance of an immortal. His conception, which of course was incestuous, parallels the cross-fertilisation of plants, and his legend, symbolises the life cycle of plants that germinate in spring, grow throughout the summer, suffer a temporary death in winter and come to life again with the return of spring. In infancy he had been dedicated to Aphrodite and placed under the care of the priestesses in the temple, where the votaries of the goddess paid him honours similar to those they paid her. As soon as he was strong enough to carry a spear, he began to hunt the wild animals that roamed free in the forests of Paphos. Aphrodite used to amuse herself watching him stalking his prey and felt proud of his exceptional skill, but was at the same time concerned about his total absorption in this activity. So she resolved to teach the adventurous youth the art of love. Disguising herself as a forest nymph, she intercepted him while he was out hunting and by artful sighs and maidenly blushes drew him to her. The ground beneath was deep in moss and lichen and as they lay down upon it, it blossomed forth in a profusion of violets. When she had sufficiently instructed him she revealed her true identity and from that time on they were inseperable, to the extent that Aphrodite began to neglect her duties on Mount Olympus. Together they would roam the woods and ridges, accompanied by their hunting dogs, in pursuit of game and when they had caught as many as they wanted they would lie down and she would begin instruction anew. This scandalised the more austere deities, who considered her dalliance unbecoming and soon their malicious gossip was half way round the world and could not help but come to her attention. This angered her and when Clio, the muse of History, reproached her in person, she lost patience and retaliated by firing in the muse a passion for King Pierus of Macedonia, a passion which resulted in Clio's pregnancy. The child conceived through this spite-induced afair, Hyacinthus, was fated to be killed quite unintentionally by his lover Apollo, who then turned him into a flower. Aphrodite and Adonis kept up their liaison in the face of growing disapproval and the jealousy of her former lovers. Among these last, Ares, the God of War, was especially envious and he swore to take revenge on the young mortal. He began by assuming the shape of a wild boar and terrorising the district of Paphos, killing and maiming the inhabitants with such brutal savagery that news of his horrendous deeds soon penetrated every corner of the hitherto peaceful island. Adonis could hardly resist such a challenge: his hunting instincts fully aroused, and ignoring Aphrodite's forbodings, he took up shield and spear and set out to conquer the scourge of his countrymen.

He made his way to the hillside where the boar was known to dwell and here he beheld a terrible sight; a field strewn with macabre remains of unfortunate people. He looked around to see if he could recognize anyone he knew, but all the bodies were so mutilated that it was impossible to tell one man from another. Perhaps for the first time in his life Adonis was frightened for he had never seen such destruction, but taking his courage in both hands he walked boldly towards the largest clear space he could find and there he roared out his challenge to the boar. As if the creature needed any warning; he had been observing the young hunter's movements for some time from the inconspicuous entrance of his lair. He calculated the distance between Adonis and himself and having formed his strategy, charged at the youth with great speed, raising a thick cloud of dust around him. Adonis whose eye normally as keen as an eagle's was blinded and when he came to throw his spear it was as though he were aiming at a crowd of phantoms. The boar, intent upon his course had only to make the slightest movement, no more than a twitch, to avoid the hurtling weapon and within an instant Adonis lay trampled and gored among the decaying dead. Ares bowed over his wounded rival and for a while could not help but admire the young man's beauty, but a vengeful satisfaction soon overtook this feeling and he departed without making any effort to save him. An owl who had witnessed these events quickly carried the news to Aphrodite, who rushed, griefstricken to the scene. Already from the distance she could hear the dying groans of Adonis, and she wheeled her chariot, drawn by giant swans, this way and that through the trees and mountains of Cyprus. But by the time she arrived it was too late to stem the flow of blood. She laid him on a bed of lettuce and exerted all her divine strength and knowledge to revive him. In vain, for even immortals are powerless against death. As soon as his spirit fled from the body, the fields, in sympathy, dried up and the grass turned pale and the trees shed their leaves and ripening fruits.

Aphrodite was overcome with grief. She wept for many days and nights without ceasing so that even the sternest of the gods were moved and tried to comfort her, but she was inconsolable. Eventually she decided to plead with Zeus for the return of her lover, and he, being acquainted with her sorrow promised to ask Persephone, the queen of the underworld, if she was willing to release young Adonis. Put Persephone had herself fallen in love with the beautiful youth and was loth to let him go. When Zeus saw how deeply they both loved this mortal, to the extent that neither could bear to be parted from him he wisely ruled that for four months of the year Adonis could live where he pleased provided he divided the rest of his time equally between the two goddesses. And so it was done: Persephone had him for four months as was her due, and Aphrodite for eight because he preferred to spend his free time with the Goddess of Love. As a lasting memorial to her lover Aphrodite sprinkled Adonis' blood with nectar and at the touch of this liquid the blood gathered and contracted unto the shape of the flower we now call Anemone. The name comes from the Greek for "wind", for its life is short and its petals easily shaken off by the gentlest breeze. The votaries of Aphrodite stage the death and resurrection of Adonis at the beginning of Spring, which comes at different times of the year in different countries. These festivals are called the Adonia and last for two days... The first day the death of Adonis is lamented by women with wailing cries, on the second day people celebrate his resurrection with spectacular displays.

The wailing during the first day of the Adonia was meant to indicate that women shared the sorrow of their goddess, caused by the death of her lover, but also was part of an agricultural rite. Nature deities,

33

like Adonis and Aphrodite, shed tears which were necessary for the fertility of the soil; the weeping ceremony of the women had the same purpose. Similarly sowers simulated mourning Aphrodite when they cast seed in the soil "to die" so that it might spring up as corn.

The hymns chanted by the women mourners of Paphos were numerous and long. Most of them originate in Babylonia and were introduced into Paphos by king Cinyras, others by Phoenician colonists and merchants. One of the hymns went as follows:

> *He has gone, he has gone to the bossom of the earth,*
> *And the dead are numerous in the land...*
> *Men are filled with sorrow, they stagger by day in gloom*
> *In the month of your name*
> *You have gone on a journey that grieves your people...*

A hymn sang in the temple refers to the slaying of Adonis:

> *Beloved of Aphrodite, the temple is empty*
> *wise shepherd, Lord of knowledge,*
> *why have they slain you?*
> *The spirit of life has left the meadows*
> *we wail for the flowers without aroma*
> *we wail for the corn without ears*
> *we wail for the sheep which bring forth no more*
> *we wail for the black hair people, they create no more.*

As the day went on the number of mourners increased with new arrivals from villages around Paphos and the ceremenies became increasingly rowdy and hysterical. The village women who liked to upset the town authorities marched through the streets with bare breasts and dishevelled hair, shouting obscenities, and tearing their clothes to shreds. Among them were bands of musicians playing tympana and pipes.

The second day of the Adonia was more joyful. People celebrated the resurrection of Adonis with animal sacrifices, feasting and praying.

END OF THE CINYRAID DYNASTY

According to Anacreon, the poet of Ionia, King Cinyras lived for one hundred and sixty years, dying in peace amidst great wealth. He was buried in the Temple of Aphrodite which he himself had helped build and is now remembered as one of the few people privileged enough to have seen and speken with the goddess in person, and have been a recipient of her generosity. His successors who carried the title Adonis, in memory of his brave son, were considered the official lovers of Aphrodite and were also to be buried in the Temple, the whole dynasty lasting over a thousand years. The decline of the dynasty begun at the time of Alexander the Great.

When Alexander swept into Syria and Palestine he received military assistance from all the Cypriot kings except Necocles of Paphos. Nicocles ruled over a theocracy and he refused to help a man who seemed bent on destroying states very similar to his own Paphos, in the name of Hellenism. Alexander never forgave Nicocles for this and soon after occupying the port of Tyre he accused him of corruption and had him replaced by a puppet ruler Alynomus, whose claims to the title were guite spurious, having been nothing but a gardener all his life. This episode illustrates the contempt in which Alexander held his enemies and provides also a measure of his power. But human life is short and Alexander's particularly so. As soon as he died the old dynasty reasserted its precedence and Timarchus Cinyras took over the kingdom, to be succeeded two years later by his son Nicocles II who ruled for a further ten years before the city fell to the Ptolemies when he committed suicide.

The capture of Paphos by the Ptolemies was a catastrophy that may well have been avoided. After the death of Alexander the Great in 295 B.C. two of his former generals, Antigonos, who ruled Syria, and Ptolemy the ruler of Egypt, laid claim to the island of Cyprus. Following a great deal of intrigue, Ptolemy landed on Cyprus with a large army and overran all the cities except Paphos, which he decided to spare, for he was sensitive to the religious feelings of the populace. This state of precarious independance was not to last however, for it came to the conqueror's notice that Nicocles Cinyras, the Paphian King, was secretly dealing with Antigonos, his rival. Ptolemy took grave offence at this breach of faith and in punishment sent two of his most capable commanders, Argeos and Kallicrates, to capture and execute the king. Their forces surrounded the city and Nicocles was ordered to commit suicide. At first he tried to save his life by profuse apologies promises of allegiance, tributes and so forth, but soon he saw that his case was hopeless, he gathered up the remnants of his pride and withdrew into his chamber and there hung himself, the last of the Cinyraid Kings of Cyprus. His brothers then locked the gates of the palace, set fire to it and slew themselves. Over the crackling of flames and the screaming of frightened

35

women, the Ptolemies shouted to those remaining alive that they were prepared to grant safe conduct to the Royal women and children. They might have taken up this offer had not queen Axiothea, maddened with grief and beyond reason, insisted that her relatives refuse outright; so all the women followed her onto the roof of the palace where, watched by a crowd of citizens from the square below, they stabbed first their children, then themselves to death until only the bereaved queen was left standing. She strode furiously about the little pile of corpses lamenting each one until, seizing on a large discarded sword she too drove the blade deep into her heart and fell into the flames that by now had engulfed all parts of the building. The fire was eventually subdued but there were no bodies found and it was up to the scattered remnants of the royal family to form a council and choose in the traditional way, the eldest among them to be the high priest of the goddess. But the power had gone, the only office that remained to this man consisted of purely religious duties for the Ptolemies abolished the city kingdoms and placed the whole island under the rule of a governor; and thus it continued for another three hundred years until the Roman conquest in 58 B.C.

This last named Nicocles II had introduced a number of reforms in order to appease the aggressive Hellenism of Alexander's successors. He had built a temple to Hera and cultivated the worship of Apollo, both deities more representative of new rather than traditional Cypriot ways. His coins represented Aphrodite on one side and Apollo on the other. He had combined the priesthood of Aphrodite with that of Hera in spite of the fact that the two goddesses were legendary rivals. In effect these two strange gods were usurping the goddess of the island and it was no suprise to many people when the king came to a bad end. But Nicocles is remembered even now; a small village standing on the original site of Paphos bears his name.

Eleven years after the conquest of Cyprus by the Romans, Mark Antony gave the island to Cleopatra as a gift. Cleopatra, like all the Ptolemaic queens of Egypt, considered herself to be the personification of Aphrodite so in this respect the gift was perfectly appropriate but the arrangement lasted only a few years. When Cleopatra and her lover committed suicide in 31 B.C. the Romans took control once more and gave the priesthood of Paphos to the local branch of the Ptolemy family as compensation for the loss of their realm. The religious power of the new High Priest extended over the whole island but was centred on Paphos.

36

With the appointment of the first Ptolemy High Priest the association of the Cinyras family with the temple, which lasted for a thousand years, was terminated. The Ptolemies administered the temple faithfully and in prosperity until the Christian era.

In the 4th century A.D. paganism was proscribed throughout the Byzantine Empire. The great temple at Paphos was converted into a Christian church, only to be destroyed by marauding Saracens some five hundred years later. When this church was rebuilt the sacred Black Stone, the chair of Aphrodite, was cemented into the wall. It can now be seen in the Cyprus Museum, but before it was transfered there only a few years ago, childless women used to visit the wall, believing that if they touched the godess' chair, they would be cured of their sterility.

For over a thousand years, from the time of king Cinyras until the Christian era, the temple had remained a centre of intellectual and spiritual life, a meeting place for people of all countries, its fame ensuring that Aphrodite would forever be associated with Cyprus.

SACRED PROSTITUTION IN ANCIENT PAPHOS

Cinyras had introduced sacred prostitution as part of the cult of Aphrodite and the temple in Paphos was famous for the large number of its beautiful priestesses. There were precedents for this, for in ancient times prostitution was a profession free of social or moral stigma. In deed it was believed to fulfil a social need and brothels existed throughout the Greek world. Many public figures were associated with prostitutes and the Athenian courtesan Phryne was commemorated with a statue at Delphi, the most sacred place in all Greece. The religious aspect of harlotry was based on the belief that anyone having intercourse with the goddess in charge of procreation or with one of her priestesses would be rewarded generously.

The priestesses of Aphrodite in Paphos, whose function was not entirely sexual, were trained in the complex rules of sacrifice, prayer and purification. They played prominent parts during the Aphrodisia festival and took part in sacrificial feasts. When public prayers were offered to the goddess their participation in large numbers was considered essential. Priestesses were not required to possess any special qualities other than the willingness to carry out their duties concientiously. Some self-employed prostitutes worked in a part-time capacity in the temple and were allowed to keep part of the money they had earned there.

The usual source of prospective priestesses was the lowest class of temple ministrants, called the sacred servants. Some of these servants were bought by the temple, others were dedicated to it by their parents when they were children. Their numbers ran into thousands of both sexes and all were at the High Priest's beck and call. Normally they would be put to domestic or agricultural work, but some of the women were creamed off and trained as priestesses.

Another source of priestesses were the wealthy pilgrims with their slave girls. In those times men always sought to gain the affection of their gods through bribery and to this effect the rich liked to buy beautiful girls on the slave market and dedicate them to Aphrodite. In return the goddess was expected to repay the kindness and for this reason, at the end of the dedication ceremony, the donors stood up with arms outstretched and palms turned expectantly as though in the act of receiving a present.

All women in Paphos had to serve in the temple for one day a year during a festival celebrating the reunion of Aphrodite with her lover Adonis who returned from the dead at the beginning of every spring. The daughters of king Cinyras himself served the goddess in this way—an indication that the rule embraced all women of a certain age, irrespective of social class. The girls wore special head scarves and sat in a line inside the temple waiting to be chosen by a man. Men paraded up and down inspecting the girls and when one of them took their fancy they threw a silver coin in her lap and claimed her in the name of the goddess. The girls had no right to refuse a man and the silver coin went to the temple. The idea behind this rite was to immitate the reunion of Aphrodite with Adonis. For the same reason a sacred marriage between the high priest and a priestess was performed in the temple and was consumated in a chamber decorated with greenery. These rites pleased the goddess of fertility who responded by activating the creative forces in nature so that the crops grew, the fruits matured and the animals were able to reproduce their kind.

In early antiquity, when women in Paphos were still forbidden to marry unless they had first had intercourse with a stranger, all girls had to act as priestesses temporarily, until they were relieved of their maidenhood. In those days Cypriot men considered the act of deflowering a virgin dangerous and the temples of Aphrodite became crowded with girls waiting for foreign pilgrims. It is not surprising that some women waited for years before they attracted a lover.

It is wrong to assume that all the temples of Aphrodite were palaces of licence and debauchery and that all her priestesses were part-time prostitutes. There were temples dedicated to Aphrodite where the priestesses had to be virgins and if any of them broke her vows of chastity she was punished severely. On one occasion a priestess was buried alive. Men who accused a virgin priestess of Aphrodite without justification were charged before a priest-judge who could sentence them to have their foreheads branded.

The office of the high priest was not open to women but some priestesses, with special intuitive talents, rose to become oracles of the temple. These girls, being the main channel through which the goddess spoke, were extremely influential and were consulted by government officials and the military, as well as by private citizens. They spoke in the name of Aphrodite after having been stimulated by some device into an ecstatic condition. The knowledge that matters of life and death depended on their advice ensured that oracles would take their duties seriously. The vagueness of some of their answers was not designed merely to cover themselves in case of failure but was due also to their reluctance to commit themselves lightly. If one is to judge from their popularity they seemed to have exercised their duties well and to the benefit of those who sought their advice.

SACRIFICES

Ancient Cypriots were deeply religious people, constantly dependent on heir gods most of whom were nature divinities. They seemed to be able to communicate quite easily with the supernatural, the usual method employed being that of sacrifice. These were regularly conducted in Aphrodite's temples. At Paphos the main altar was reserved for "pure" offerings, that is to say those which did not invole slaughter but this was not so elsewhere in the building. The function of the sacrifice determined the nature of the thing offered; for instance at the beginning to each new cultivating season the goddess' aid was implored with bloodless oblations such as honey cakes, wine, fruit or vegetables. When crops had been gathered in, the same sacrifices were made as a token of gratitude. Normally they were placed on the altar or somewhere near it but other times they were thrown into the sea. Their contact either with the altar holding the sacred fire or with the sea in which Aphrodite was born, sanctified the offerings which were eaten afterwards. It was the belief that solid matter represented the body of the goddess while the liquids symbolised her blood.

Sacrificial animals were supposed to be inhabited by good spirits and so their innards, the liver, the lungs and the heart were first to be roasted. They were to be eaten while the spirit was still present in them. Then other parts of the carcass were cooked to provide a common feast for the goddess and her people. Normally male animals were offered to gods and female ones to goddesses, but this rule was not followed at Paphos where Aphrodite would only accept males. Whatever the sacrifice, were it ram, bull or swine, it had to be in perfect health for abnormality displeased the goddess and there were severe penalties for those who offered faulty specimens.

Sacrifices were sponsored by the city authorities as well as by individuals who wanted some special favour or wished to consult the oracle of the temple. Public figures leaving office were compelled by tradition to sacrifice an animal to Aphrodite as a gesture of gratitude for blessings they had enjoyed during their term.

All sacrifices were festive occasions with a diversity of entertainments financed by those who wished to carry favour with the goddess and as most sacrifices took place in the festival season there was a great appetite for feasting, singing, dancing and athletic competitions. Some of the songs that have been preserved reflect the prevailing high spirits and easy familiarity that existed between the goddess and her worshippers. Because the goddess was believed to participate in the feast in person an empty chair was kept for her at the end of the nobles' table next to the high priest.

As to the sacrifices themselves they were preceded by a purification ceremony: a jar of water was sanctified by contact with the altar, the knife to be used was put in a basket along with some corn and carried round it. Then both priest and worshippers washed their hands in the water and the body of the victim was sprinkled with the corn. Then followed the dedication. The officiating priest cut off some of the animal's hair and praying all the while threw it into the sacred fire. This prayer, in the event of a public sacrifice, was declaimed aloud, and the reason for the sacrifice made clear. But if the sacrifice was made by an individual, and was of a personal nature, likely to ambarass him, the prayer was whispered. When this was completed the priestesses and the women among the participants officially entreated Aphrodite's presence. The size of the flame produced by the burnt hair was an indication of the goddess's favour and indicated whether the petition would be granted or not. If it was of the correct size the victim was decked with garlands and led to the altar where its head was drawn back so that its face was turnèd to the sky, and its throat was then slit by a priest using the sanctified knife. Powerful animals were first stunned with a few skilful blows from the blunt end of an axe for too much struggling would have been indecorous. The animal was then skinned and cut to pieces, some of which were wraped in fat and burned on the sacred fire while libations of wine were poured over them. The burnt pieces and the wine, were believed to be consumed by the goddess. The priest who conducted the sacrifice was entitled to the hide and one of the legs of each animal but the assistant who struct the animal was not allowed to eat any of it and was paid a fee instead. If any meat was left over after the feast people were allowed to take it home.

One did not have to be wealthy in order to find a suitable sacrifice. Some offerings were modest in value and easy to come by—sparrows, flowers, little clay statuettes, incense, or even hair. The queen of Egypt, Berenice, vowed to give her hair to the goddess if her husband returned safely from a dangerous expedition. When he returned victorious her locks were placed in the temple of Aphrodite but soon afterwards disappeared and the astromomer Conon reported that Zeus had carried them away and had formed a constellation of stars out of them.

It appears that human sacrifices were offered in certain places. At Salamis and Curium for example human victims were presented annually: other towns resorted to it in extreme sircumstances. These were demanded by Aphrodite as vergeance for some great sin committed by the inhabitants of a town. When a city was threatened with catastrophy, human sacrifices were sometimes offered voluntarily in order to avert it. Corpses have been found alongside certain kinds of altars with drains in them presumably to allow the blood to run off which may have been sacrifices of this type—on the other hand the corpes may have been those of captured enemy soldiers used for that purpose. At Lapithos, in Northern Cyprus, skeletons of men bound hand and foot were discovered at the entrances of tombs, possibly slaves that had been sacrificed on the death of their masters, and who were intended to serve as doorkeepers or scapegoats.

These practices where brought into Cyprus by Teucer at the end of the Trojan war. He founded the city of Salamis, where once a year a human victim, led by youths, was made to run three times round the altar of Aphrodite where-upon the priest thrust a spear through his throat. The corpse was then trown on to a fire and burnt to ashes. Such victims were supposed to atone for the collective sins of the city populace and to deliver them from perils of disease, famine or the wrath of the gods. However, from an early age human conscience revolted against such cruelty and the rite was changed in various ways. In Curium they justified the act by selecting a criminal (that is, somebody no longer fit to live) as victim and he was thrown over a cliff into the sea. At Amathus they avoided the issue by sacrificing strangers only to Zeus Xenios but the custom offended Aphrodite and the offenders were changed into bulls. In other towns they simply simulated a human sacrifice or they replaced human victims with animals. The practice was abolished during the reign of the Roman Eperor Hadrian. King Deiphilus of Salamis was the first of the Greek leaders to substitute oxen. It is interesting that oxen should have been considered suitable, because to this day

Cypriot peasants attribute human qualities to the creature and many of them regard consumption of beef as cannibalism.

DIVINATION

In the course of time the temple of Aphrodite in Paphos accumulated a mass of information dealing with every augural phenomenon. This information was documented and classifed and was passed on from one generation of priests to the next. The rites connected with divination were jealously guarded. Consultations with the oracle were held during festivals or on Fridays, which being the day of Aphrodite was deemed to be lucky.

One of the methods used was to pour oil (provided by suppliants) on to cold water and then read the course of future events in the shapes made by the separated oil. Another method was hepatoscopy which means the examination of the liver of a sacrificed animal. The direction, size and colour of the veins were the crucial factors and were interpreted with reference to their resemblance to objects or events: Those on the right hand side were favourable, those on the left unfavourable. The Paphian oracles were very highly regarded which would seem to indicate that their forcasts were generally accurate, a reasonable supposition if we bear in mind that these oracles were in a unique advantageous position to gather confidential information. After all temples were meeting places for all ranks of society. People explained their situation quite comprehensively before asking for advice, then again, the psychological effect of a favourable forecast often ensured that it would come true. However on occassion the pronouncements of the oracles were so obscure and mysterious that they had to be interpreted by a priest which gave an opportunity to those in charge to reflect and take extra advise on difficult questions.

Apart from the official oracles there were freelance magicians who attended the festivals and hawked their talents in the market place as seers, interpreters of dreams or healers and a great deal of semi-religious magic took place with the purpose of compelling the goddess to respond to somebody's request. Often the motives that lay behind these efforts were malicious: revenge, spite, greed etc. Alternatively they were used to excorcise evil spirits or to insure someone against a spell.

The popularity of oracles was partly due to superstition. The Greek

43

Cypriots believed that unusual events in nature were omens, and when these occured they asked an oracle who had the necessary training to explain their meaning. Their attitude to natural phenomena is understandable considering that their gods represented the various forces in nature. Omens were read in cloud formations, in the behaviour of animals and in many other ways. Human, animal, plant and geological monstrosities, as well as freak weather conditions were signs that a god had been angered and had to be placated with a sacrifice.

CHAPTER THREE

· THE TRAVELS OF BRONTEAS

FESTIVALS

I am back to Aphrodisium again. I must admit I like the place more and more despite its filth. A disgusting smell of stale food and offal permeates my room. Nobody notices it here. If you mention it to them they look at you with startling eyes. But with all the festivities everyone is so cheerful it is hard to remain angry or even disgusted for long.

Yesterday I saw the pigs that are to be offered for sacrifice tomorrow. All twelve looked in excellent condition. (In a town like this it is scarcely surprising!) I hope it turns out well for them though. The last two years have produced rather poor harvests.

Having walked for a week in delightful weather I am as brown as an Egyptian, my skin hardened (especially the soles of my feet), my weight reduced, and my strength doubled. One really should take more exercise.

I am a little surprised with Idalium. I had heard something about Idalian procedure but was not prepared for this. Let me start at the beginning. I arrived on Monday at about lunch time, so naturally the first place I inquired after was an inn. A slim and elegant young man offered to direct me to a suitable place and I walked along with him through some groves until we came to a large house set in a small but extremely ornate garden. 'This', he spoke in light melodious accents, 'is my house. You are welcome to share a meal with us'. So I followed him inside. The house too was decorated, liberally strewn with flowers, pitchers of wine, small statuettes. It was all very delicious but somehow queer. Imagine my surprise when, as my host called out some names, there appeared at various doorways the strangest assortment of creatures: A being whose limbs were covered in strips of light grey fur and from whose snouted head there protruded two enormous ears; another smeared in grease and paint, wearing pink garments, a piggish mask and from behind whom there peeped a curling tight little piggish tail. Was I dreaming? Then a third creature appeared. He was less startling than the others though in his own way just as queer. A man, sporting a full grown black beard and thunderous eyebrows, he slunk into the room, attired in a filmy female dress and exuding a most heady perfume, he, seeing my confusion, hastened to reassure me. In a masculine voice (I believe he had a cold) be explained that all this masquerade was part of the Spring Festival. His two daughters, normally charming creatures he assured me, were assuming the identities of a rabbit and a pig respectively. He himself dressed as his wife and his wife (the elegant young man who had brought me here) was wearing the clothes of a man. Of course when he said this the whole thing fell into place. The idea of changing sexes is not after all uncommon. I believe we had at one time practised it ourselves but the custom died out.

But to cut the matters short I enjoyed an axcellent meal with good wine and found accommodation. Having expressed a desire to participate in the ceremony I was provided with an old costume of the mother's, anointed with perfumes, and was teased and petted by the daughters. My host then said the necessary prayers and the lot of us went back down to the town.

Here the festival was in full swing; people, creatures, running about doorway to doorway, laughing, singing, dancing. The family split up and I was quickly set upon by two locals who plied me with wine and scattered flower petals all over me. Don't ask me whether they were men or women! Thus the afternoon passed into a haze. I seem to remember the temple a little way out of town, incense, some bright and glorious cotumes, and indeed for a few minutes something very like a vision, a tall beautiful woman shimmering among the tree's impossible height.

After that it was bodies and limbs, beasts, birds and singing. Heaven knows where I rested. I woke in darkenss in somebody's garden. There were people scattered about here and there. It must have been early in the morning for the sky was steadily growing lighter. I sat for a while with my head in my hands, then noticed smoke rising over the nearest houses, and heard music. I wandered across to find a great bonfire and a group of musicians warming themselves, idly plucking at strings and blowing down pipes, so I joined them. Eventually they produced some food which they were generous enough to share with me, and as the sun rose a crowd gathered in various states of undress, some clutching cloaks round themselves, in their hands they held remnants of the night's costumes. Then the priests arrived. They stoked up the fire and ordered the musicians to play. Now people began dancing, quite slowly and decorously, round the flames, and as the music grew wilder they cast their costumes onto the fire. I soon got the hang of this and took off some of my own clothes (my hostess's I should say). They believe that mischievous and evil spirits inhabit people's clothes. All evil was to be burnt away. The naked body was to remain pure. The clothes were in effect atoning for last night's orgy! (Hence the disguise, it confuses the demons). I am sitting at my kind host's table now having drunk more wine than is absolutely good for me. Dare I suggest that the whole thing is only a pretence? An excuse if you like? Does the Goddess really approve? Still, the idea is rather clever.

What can I say about Tamasus? All our copper come from here. Everything that can be is made of copper, from pans to plaques and jewellery. I have even seen copper fecades and copper roofs - mostly green of course. But the chief attraction here is the Sacred Grove and the tree that produced the golden apple Aphrodite gave to Atalanta.

I saw women queueing there for consecrated fruit. The priests administer these as cure for childlessness. Apparently it is very successul. For me the place has great appeal. It is peaceful, well regulated and one does feel a kind of serenity radiating as it were from the groves.

I have been excluded from all the rites! Not for any transgression on my part, any ineligibility owing to poor preparation or lax morals, but because I am a man. The whole male population of Tamasus is excluded. So we sit here together in the market place pondering what could possibly be going on in the temple. Quite futile of course - nobody will ever know. Ah, but we may guess. There are all kinds of queer theories, most of them too disgusting to repeat, which show how little we men trust women. A part of me concurs with the general feeling. Women are less trustworthy and far more lascivious than we are.

However I am straying from the point which was one of masculine theories about female rites. Here is where the comic element comes in, for if you happen to go down to the market place as I did the other day, you will hear the most idiotic talk about not merely the rites but about the most normal features of these people's wives. The spirit is quite infectious. Everyone knows it is all lies but we sit there and laugh until we are sick and fall over backwards then become terribly gloomy until someone else starts us off again.

A liberal dose of wine helps to maintain the atmosphere. I quickly grow tired of this but the locals don't-they continue in this vein sometimes for the whole three days. More serious explanations of the women's activities involve extreme forms of sexuality, perhaps a menstruation rite and one man thought that the women were making some kind of blood sacrifice but that they were getting the victims from elsewhere. There are many plausible theories. The object of the ceremony is to increase the fertility of trees—the ostensible object at any rate. But I must not be cynical—it is merely the prevailing spirit, besides I did manage to see one part of the ritual. There is a procession that takes place in the open air and though strictly speaking we are not admitted, there is nothing to stop us watching from a respectful distance. The women emerged from the temple in strict formation. It was all very orderly. Most wore white but some were dressed in deep red. The one in front carried a small torch.

They then took a mazy path around the fruit trees, singing a very quiet song whose wards we could not make out, especially when they were circumscribing the far end of the garden. However when they approached us we did get a decent view of the parade and it became obvious that most of them were carrying some object of medium size that appeared on careful scrutiny to be a stone or wooden image of the phallus. It is amazing how a ritual becomes tiresome when one is not taking part oneself. They continued in this manner for some time, then they sat down in the centre, first placed their images by a particularly large tree, and after a while they rose and began walking again. I got bored and started walking home. As I passed some houses near the market place I was accosted by two girls who obviously had better things to do than attend religious ceremonies. What with one thing and another I took up their offer. They had not been short of trade the last few days.

The next day I was on my way down to the market when I saw Adrian, an aquantance from my home town, on the other side of the street, puffing and sweating his eyes swivelling in his head, obviously looking out for me. What could I do? I tried to duck down a passage but only succeeded in drawing attention to myself. He was after me in a flash. I pretended not to see him and hurried on by a roundabout way to the market on the chance that I might lose him in a crowd. Vain hope! Our chasing game lasted only a few minutes then he was upon me. Of course I had to pretend to be pleased to see him: 'What a delightful surprise' etc. He knew very well that I had attempted to escape him, but refused to confront me with the fact. He in turn pretended to be just as surprised as I was. 'Fancy meeting you here. I only came down to do some business. I am on the point of pulling off one of the biggest deals of my life. In copper. That's where the money is to be made but there is one small difficulty. On my way here, dreadful event! I was robbed by some bandits, leaving me rather short—nothing I cant't easily raise once I get home of course—but inconvenient under the circumstances. But the Gods are kind. Who would have thought that here, in a foreign country I would find my dear comrade (I don't know what he means by that), Bronteas, who is known for his kindness, and for being the one man in Cyprus who is never short of ready cash. Here is what I propose' he continued in one breath, 'if just for once you cover my expenses here, I'll cut you in on the deal. Of course the robbers will be captured and executed, some part of my money will be recovered, and when everything is sorted out we shall both be rich. Or at least comfortable. Well, what do you say?'

I had to think quickly. 'Well, I can't promise anything, old friend, you always have exaggerated the extent of my wealth-but,' and here I pretended to consider, 'if what you say is true—and the deal does sound attractive—I'll do what I can to help you. You haven't mentioned the precise sum and I am not in the habit of carrying all my money round town with me, but here's what I'll do. If you meet me back here this afternoon I shall be able to provide you with some money and a letter of credit with my family in Carpasia. That ought to satisfy everyone.' 'Alright', said he, 'see you in the afternoon'.

Needless to say I never intended to return to the arranged place but rushed off home and packed my bags. I had prepared everything and was on the point of quitting the house when Adrian turned up. I told him he was early and asked him to wait for me round the corner. I sneaked out through the back. But I hadn't got more than a few miles out of Tamasus when I came upon him sitting by the roadside, munching cakes. There was no need for explanations. I sat down with him and shared his cakes.

We are back in Tamasus. We had progressed barely a mile beyond our last post when, I stumbled against a rock, turned my ankle and impaled myself on a particularly sharp thorn that I could not for the life of me remove. Adrian tried to help but his useless flapping succeeded only in annoying me. I wrote to my wife instructing her to send our slave Phylon. I should never have travelled without him. It makes people suspicious in the first place and besides that, I have, contrary to my expectations, found myself with an increasing amount of luggage.

There was no alternative to a very painful return to Tamasus with the dubious assistance of my friend. It had grown terribly hot; the pebbles scorched my feet and I was thirsting continually. I was afraid of fever. I always have been. I loathe the way one loses control of oneself under an attack.

Adrian has been good to me. He has brought me food, news, kept me occupied with conversation, paid the bills (with my money to be sure) and has even found me a doctor. Apparently people are gathering for another festival. I hadn't realised there would be one so soon—and among the visitors are a number of medical men.

The doctor who visited me was a most disreputable looking man, his garments soiled, his skin blotchy, his teeth bad and his smell repulsive—I had a good mind to dismiss him at once but just then I suffered a shooting pain down my leg so for a moment was incapacitated and without speech. Meanwhile he had spread his large bundle out across the floor and was examining my knee with gravity, muttering to himself in a foreign dialect. 'Can't you cure him?' asked Adrian. 'That should not prove beyond my powers'. answered the other. Then he selected a large white bulb. 'Sea squill' he explained, holding it up like a conjuror at a fair. He peeled off a segment, asked for water and went out of the room, presumably to boil the thing for when he returned it was steaming. He slapped the soft remnant on the wound without so much as an apology (I was in agonies) and fastened it tightly with a strip of cloth. Once the business was over he became all affability and offered to sell us concoctions as cures for anything from the plaque to impotence. A few hours later the wound opened up and the thorn oozed out along with a deal of abscess. Doctors are such queer fellows—I've never seen one that did not look utterly untrustworthy. But the pain has gone. I can walk about my room.

I am well now and ready to move on to Citium. The festival I mentioned took place over the last three days. It was surprisingly archaic in its concentration on homosexual intercourse. Once this used to be so in Carpasia too I believe but the custom was dropped in my grandfather Philip's time. I found it difficult to take the thing as seriously as I ought to have done—for while I think such passion natural I cannot see how Aphrodite is honoured by it—surely fecundity is the point and not amusement or gratification of everday desires. The young men are treated quite violently and must submit to one or other of the priests under the pretence of resistance. There were some exceptionally attractive boys there.

The slave Phylon turned up yesterday much to my relief.

Once again I have arrived too early but as I am here I may as well look around. My leg is completely recovered so I am able to do as much walking as I wish. Phylon carries my belongings and Adrian intends leaving within a day or so, partly to take up my loan, partly to pursue some business interest in Carpasia.

I was surprised to find it raining when I arrived. The salt lake was still and dark and the rain punctured it everywhere with pock-marks, like beaten silver. Between the trees I could see a colony of ducks that seemed to extend for almost a mile. Then there were flamingoes that had cornered a little bay of their own. We made our way through the palms and into the town itself. The centre of Citium is on quite high ground and all the important temples are situated here. By the evening the rain had stopped and the sky was clearing, and a pleasant red glow lay over the whole area. We found accommodation at an inn and took the opportunity to indulge ourselves in a really fine meal prepared by the proprietor who is of Phoenician descent but employs a number of Persians. There seems to be no racial friction here at any rate. Space was rather limited and I had to share my room with two Syrians who were here on business. They were loud talkative men and quickly drew me into their conversation. They, along with some four others, appeared to be members of some delegation privately commissioned, and were keen on visiting the local brothel of which they had heard a great deal. It sounded an extremely low class kind of place to me but I agreed to accompany them on a visit.

51

It was just as I had thought, worse, and it was as well that we paid our visit after dark for I have since heard that no respectable citizen would dream of entering the place in broad daylight. At the entrance stands a statue of Aaphrodite Callipyge, well carved and extremely enticing in the way she peeks at one over her shoulder, her hindquarters pushed out and raised in invitation. I ought to mention at this point that this brothel contained not girls but men. Inside it was dark for the torches they used were small and placed at long intervals. On closer inspection the ornaments supporting the torches turned out to be cast-iron male figures engaged in various forms of copulation. We were conducted round by a pretty boy whose long hair was ornately curled and hung down past his shoulders. He spoke in a low whisper but would now and then erupt into coarse laughter when dwelling on some detail of the decoration. He made much of the Syrians and showed by his conversation that he was well acquainted with Syrian politics and sexual habits. However I noticed that he cast his warmest glances at me. The murals also showed scenes of homosexual revelry whose details do not vary enough to call for a full description. Everything was exaggerated of course as one would expect; a mixture of the impossibly graceful and the outrageously comical. Fat men with tiny acrobats, tiny men with gross and larded prostitutes, two mascular fellows treating the whole thing as though it were some strenuous gymnastic exercise. There were captions to many of these but I cannot remeber one off hand. Outside a warm wind had sprung up and every so often I was caught in a pleasant draught between two windows. My Syrian acquaintances were soon conducted to the rooms of their choice and I being unable to name my pleasure was left to talk with the boy. We walked around the temple together. He rather resented the low standing of his profession (the locals call them dogs) and indeed wished he had been born a woman so as to escape this odium. I consoled him by pointing out that he was very young and very beautiful and these things were not to be despised. At this he cheered up 'We are all under the goddess's protection", he said and we continued talking till the early hours of the morning.

I walked around the harbour. What a cosmopolitan gathering it is: the costumes alone provide a kind of gazetteer. A bright and sunny day, the sun sparkling off the water, the surf thick and very white, triremes, quinqueremes, small fishing boats, bannered masts and sails, curious prows with foreign inscriptions. On the promenade one hears many strange languages; ugly bulbous words; coughing, scratching noises;

musical speeches and languages that seemed to be like ours but turn out to be indecipherable. The place is crowded too with beggars and cripples and packages of all sorts. I saw one man fall into the water. He must have been drowned for I did not see him surface again. No-one bothered. The city has done well under the Phoenicians.

Adrian departed today in high spirits. He has joined up with a party of travellers heading East so he has some entertainment—he may even ride for they had a number of horses between them. The lovely boy is fickle.

Being tired of Citium and the weather having taken a turn for the better I decided to climb the mountain of Aphrodite nearby and visit its famous temple. What a steep climb it is! The path is very narrow and twists and winds in the most awkward way between briars and nettles, over loose shingle and patches of slippery moss, so that one is quite exhausted by the time one reaches the top: it is impossible, as you may imangine, in the winter to any but the most practised mountaineer. However there are many consolations once you have begun for all along the path, by every tree, bush or outcrop you will find some sort of shrine: even rocks and the larger stones to say nothing of the shallow little caves pitting the mountainside, forming natural niches and hollows, are consecrated by priests and have altars improvised whereon are arranged the customary offerings of beans, almonds, oil or what you will, besides crudely formed wax or clay images of diseased pilgrims whose ailments are indicated by abnormalities in the relevant limbs or organs. There are some with wounds, some with swellings, several toothless. I myself stopped at one of these and moulded a likeness out of damp earth, giving it a cleft knee in memory of my recent injury. Then both Phylon and I stopped to pray; I in thanks-giving for my cure, Phylon for a sick mother; all this to the accompaniment of bird song (they sing prettily among the trees and bushes and appear very tame). Turning away I barely avoided putting my hand on a scorpion, which—the avoidance I mean not the scorpion itself—I take for a good omen, and the creature scuttled back into an overturned jar among a group of neglected statuettes.

It is a good place for prayer. Firstly, it is private: no-one can approach you without making his presence known some time before he arrives, for the ascent is steep and much noise is unavoidable; one is always breaking branches, dislodging stones or upsetting other people's offerings. Thus your pleas go unheard, irrevokable, save by divine agency. Secondly, being high above the rest of the world you can feel detached from your daily cares and appear to yourself somehow more than a man, fitter company for gods and goddesses. Thindly, it is good to pray where many have prayed before, to feel the stones themselves sanctified by centuries of touching, or to enter a cave containing echoes of voices long dead: men of state, commoners, women and boys, old hags fatter than Silenus, probably wheezing and out of breath. It is a strange feeling. Did not Hesiod learn singing on a mountain?

Attaining the summit we found a group of visitors who had arrived some time ago, delegates of local farming communities, who were taking part in a water ritual, the object of which was the induction of seasonal rain. Since we had just had a day of delicious warm drizzle, it may safely be assumed that either they or a previous group had met with success. However I felt it a duty to act as the impromptu representative of my own town and joined with them in their prayers. The climax of the ceremony is spectacular and rather moving. The priest sprinkled our heads with consecrated water (this is at the altar after due offerings have been made) then we were led in procession around the temple and down to the cliff-edge, a sheer drop of frightening proportions, where the priest took what was left of the water and poured it with stylised gestures into the abyss below. We watched it fall as long as our eyes could follow it. The following day we had the interpretation of omens and detailed forecasts of rain or drought.

We have been here for close on a week now, much against our inclination, since that party of farmers that I mentioned with regard to the water ceremony was attacked and robbed by a group of bandits not a mile hence. One man returned to tell of murder and all kinds of violence, his own appearance bearing witness to the truth of his account. Apparently the farmers had hardly stepped off the mountain when they were assaulted by a band of bandits armed with spears and short-swords. One man was immediately killed, the rest taken into captivity, our fugitive managing to escape, not without conspicuous damage, after a successful struggle with two of the bandits. The priests here believe that this is a newly formed band, or perhaps one that has migrated hence from another district, for they could not recognize them from the man's description. However, they add, there is nothing unusual in this, there are frequent raids in the area, but the criminals never encroach on the mountain itself for fear of divine retribution.

This was three days ago and despite the presence of such a force there has been a steady trickle of pilgrims to the temple, but individuals rather than groups. These have been people who were ignorant of the situation and one must suppose they slipped through because the robbers deemed them not worth the trouble of fleecing. Yesterday though, the remannts of another group arrived with tales of pillage and butchery so there is no reason to feel safe. All this has led to a curious situation. The temple is so crowded that there is little room to move for none will leave now but waits here until reports arrive either of the bandits' capture or of their departure. How tiresome it is! The priests continue with their ceremonies as if nothing had happened, the gifts pile up on the altar, conversation grows stale and we are all very bored. Sometimes the priests remove some of the offerings; fruit and corn and such to the cellar, the statues to an enormous cave on the east side of the mountain. These can be very interesting I suppose, and among the bulls, monsters and human figures I came across a beautifully carved group of horned centaurs with snakes entwined about their necks. The hands of the centaurs were raised in adoration of Aphrodite who is their goddess. Even the robbers respect her it seems for there have been reports of them praying among the shrines.

We had been advised by a number of priests on which was the best route to take and they also provided us with a pair of old swords and a long curved knife, quite handsomely preserved. This descent was if anything more tortuous than our coming hence. Our legs were scratched raw by the time we were at the bottom. As this was early morning the bird song was particularly loud which helped cover up the noise we were making. Once at the foot of the mountain we were to look out for certain landmarks (unmistakeable they assured us) which would steer us clear of the area supposed to be occupied by the bandits. Apart from a few personal documents and very little money I had left all our luggage with the high priest so that, were we seen we might appear less of a temptation. One moves very slowly when one is unacquainted with the terrain and our constant debates on which were the genuine landmarks and which not slowed us down still further. I don't believe we had progressed above two miles by mid morning, yet we were hopeful that we had eluded them, for neither did we hear nor see anything remotely connected with humanity. But we were wrong. As we rounded a clump of trees we came upon a solitary horse tied up and champing the dry grass. He snorted and stamped when he caught sight of us, then two men, one of whom was leading another horse emerged from behind some bushes. We had heard them of course before they came into view and hid among the trees. From their appearance we were left in no doubt that these men were members of the gang; they were encumbered with s·vords. Suffice to say, they being alert and trained to open life, we were noticed and set upon with shouts loud enough to rouse every ruffian in Cyprus, so that I gave up all hope of life and determined to defend myself to the inevitable end. Now I could not pretend that Phylon and I (however useful we were with a sword) would have been able to overcome men like these in combat not at all suited to our more formal style, but my dreams proved good prophets. It turned out that one of the robbers was in fact already injured and badly handicapped by having his fighting hand swathed in bandages. Phylon threw his own small knife at him and I hacked off the other arm while Phylon occupied his companion, then we both set about the remaining one until we had managed to sufficiently wound him too, though powerful man as he was he inflicted a quite severe injury on Phylon in the process. But Phylon showed admirable courage and I set him on the calmer looking horse, taking the other for myself and we rode off Heaven knows where, possibly right into their arms, but in the vague direction indicated by the priests. Soon we could hear behind us the sound of horses and men and it became obvious that unless we did something unexpected we would be caught. Now we had been riding alongside a small stream, so we quickly dismounted and set our horses off while we crossed over and stumbled away among the trees. Presumably the robbers must have ridden on for we were not followed and in time came upon an old inn, where we asked to be sheltered, for Phylon was bleeding quite badly now and it was all I could do to support him and prevent the blood leaving a clear trail for our pursuers.

We remained long enough to bandage poor Phylon's wound and to use what money we had left as security for the loan of a fresh pair of horses and a guide to escort us safely to Amathus.

Amathus is a most attractive place and I have time on my hands while Phylon recovers. Furthermore there is a festival due to be celebrated soon. First let me stress the antiquity of the city, indeed the fact impresses itself upon one at every turn; from the very trees on the adjacent hillside, the olives and carobs, whose trunks are wider than anywhere else that I had seen previously, to the buildings, gates and walls decorated with martial reliefs, the groves, the shrines and relics; all of which combine to provide an air as ancient as our legends. There is a reverse side to the coin of course: the poorer civil quarters are a disgrace, narrow dark and fouled by animals and humans alike. But it would not do to dwell on these things among such a wealth of grand and beautiful objects, chief among which is the temple of Aphrodite Amathusia. This is large enough to be seen from every part of the city, having a tower seven storeys high that represents the seven zones of the planets as well as the seven zones of the earth. I was privileged enough to be shown round this edifice by one of the attendant priests, the friendliest of men, yet not without due dignity, who obviously took great pride in his post, anticipating every question with a, "But you are about to ask..." and thence proceeding to tales and explanations that I wish I had the wit to remember. What did I see? Some parts I could not be shown for they were reserved for the use of the high priest, but the records library and the city archives were pointed out to me with some enthusiasm. I was impressed by the thoroughgoing symbolism of the arrangement; for everything there was a reason or precedent; no article of furniture, no image was superfluous. Perhaps it was the very wealth of coordinated detail that leaves me now a little uncertain as to the order of my impressions (for I have not the conceit to call them any more than impressions). If I may make a profane comparison I am like a man who is found laughing at some joke yet cannot for the life of him repeat the story that brought him to this state.

The priests and priestesses are provided with seperate dwellings adjacent to the temple though some do actually join on to the main building. These are sumptuously furnished and decorated, unlike at Aphrodite Akrea where the priests had little more than holes to sleep in, and are themselves surrounded by smaller temples in the sacred enclosure, which are dedicated to various gods. On the ground floor of the main temple is a long hall, thickly collonaded, open to the public who may, with the assistance of the high-priest or, on occasion, one of the others, make an offering on the altar. Here are statues of Aphrodite and Adonis, the latter portrayed as an energetic hunter, the former naked save for a necklace of green and gold stones which are not only extremely beautiful and a great focus of attention, but are also credited with marvellous (and disturbing) powers: to bestow either immortality or death. This duality, which renders the necklace a frightening fascination, is rooted in the claim that Hephaistus himself forged it as a wedding present to Harmonia, Aphrodite's daughter. Harmonia and every possessor of that necklace since has been dogged by disaster. The priests do not allow anyone to touch it.

I lodged near the port, overlooking a public square and from a window I could see the long pier stretching out into the harbour, studded with boats and packages and could hear people of many nations shouting instructions, and carriage wheels squeaking and rattling through the streets below.

But this square is dominated by an immense statue of Hercules the Lion-Slayer, the Colossus of Amathus, monstrous-headed, horned, bearded (the beard cut square and curly in the Assyrian fashion) and with long, rough hair. A lion's skin is knotted round his waist which is lean but muscular, and he holds in his hands the hind paws of a lioness whose head hangs down between his legs and whose mouth serves as a spout from which issues a powerful stream of clear water. Pigeons are sitting on his head and shoulders. Now a gull swoops down and frightens the pigeons away. It has a rude power which I find has a reassuring effect, especially at night when the sailors fall to brawling and gangs of youths pursue each other up and down the dark streets.

There is much quarreling between the inhabitants who may be divided into three parties. There are the usual Greeks and Phoenicians but more than half the population is made up of those people whom we call proto-Cyprians, those who by tradition are thought to be descendants of the original natives of Cyprus. They are a peculiar race that do not exist anywhere else on the island, or certainly not in any recognisable community, being squat, powerful and badly proportioned: their heads and hands are far too big. They have a language of their own and are said to indulge in human sacrifice, but no doubt that is a malicious rumour, understandable in view of their haunting appearance. In times of war they tend to side with the Phoenicians and I have been made aware of some anti-Greek feeling in the city.

The oracles and soothsayers of Amathus have a scandalously poor reputation as shown by a typical example, one Thasius, who advised the King of Egypt Busiris, to sacrifice a foreigner to Zeus in order to rid his coutry of a terrible plague. This was done much to Thasius' chagrin for the foreigner whom Busiris selected to be the victim was the soothsayer himself; and neither did the matter stop there, for the sacrifice having proved afficacious Busiris took it into his head to sacrifice any foreigner who set foot in his kingdom (what this did to trade I cannot think!). Eventually Hercules turned up and he was accorded like treatment, carried to the altar, bound hand and foot, but he had no difficulty in disentangling himself and proceeded to sacrifice Busiris and his entire family on the altar of Zeus. One may fairly describe these events as disastrous. No doubt however I shall consult my usual oracle ere I quit this place.

It has been very hot here during the last week and it was difficult to summon up enthusiasm, but I joined in with most of the activities of the festival of Fruition. One of the attractions of this festival has been a performance by a young man who convincingly imitated the cries and movements of a woman in childbirth. This relates to the myth of Theseus and Ariadne, for people here believe that after killing the Minotaur Theseus came to Amathus with Ariadne who was pregnant and that being abandonned by him here, she died in labour. According to the legend the people cared for her while she lived and after her death identified her with Aphrodite thus instituting this festival of Fruition, in memory of her pregnancy. At one point in the proceedings we threw the ashes of burnt meat on a tomb known as the Tomb of Aphrodite, in the same grove. It may seem queer to have a tomb for one of the immortals but the locals justify it by reference to the Ariadne incident above, and by their belief that the goddess had spent some time in the land of the Dead, during her search for Adonis.

It was a very well attended festival, and the groves were crowded with pilgrims and salesmen selling all manner of things from oil and pottery-ware through to confections and livestock. We (for Phylon considered himself fit enough to attend) slept the nights under the trees together with merchants and their wares. Given the climate it was the most sensible and refreshing thing to do: the town smelt awful. It was not until the third day of the festival, at noon, that people began to pack up their belongings and move on. By the evening it was almost deserted save for the numerous offerings arranged in the grove. All in all it was the most impressive experience of my journey so far.

Later I had a deadful headache and felt nasty and sluggish. It was still scorchingly hot. I was off to Paphos. Dry bread and wine for me. I hired a mule and a muleteer who looked a perfect villain. We planned to travel this way at least as far as Curium. Phylon was fit to travel and the proxenos had supplied me with a reasonable loan.

Before I left I visited a soothsayer: terribly solemn and piercing-eyed. He contemplated me for a little while then closed his eyes and wrote out the following verses. It was his prophescy:

Trust to Mule and trust to Horse
Heaven shall prepare your Course,
Safely, pilgrim, journey on
The gods shall give thee benison,
Grow in wisdom and in wealth,
Fear not thou the robber's stealth,
Nor slave, nor corpse art like to be
But shall prosper constantly.

My poor condition and the dreaful heat of the day had obliged me to hire the mule-driver in the first place - well, we trotted along at a slow pace for some seven miles, having stopped off to bathe several times (on doctor's advice), and by sunset we had reached a milestone, surrounded by a large number of smaller stones. This formed a very large mound and it was our duty to supplement the pile with a stone each: for this acts as a sort of impromptu shrine to Hermes, protector of travellers, and also, alas, of thieves. It was interesting to note by the way that some of the larger stones had maps carved into them, complete with abbreviated place names and distances. The countryside around seemed very pleasant, closeted by vines and pomegranates, and other trees whose branches twined over our heads, so I suggested to the driver that it would make a fine camp for the night. He agreed and led us down to a delightful little crevice where flowed a thin, but quite clear brook. We cooled our wine in the stream and sat down to a satisfying meal of bread, cheese and fruit. And rather too much wine. Phylon was the first to fall asleep and I must have been next. I doubt the mule-driver slept at all.

The reader could perhaps supply the end of this incident without any further information from me. Let me add however that besides the money and clothes that we were carrying, I had about me certain trinkets and souvenirs of no great material value but to which I had become rather attached, to say nothing of the presents I had accumulated for friends and relatives at home. When Phylon and I woke, almost simultaneously, we found that literally everything had gone; the driver the animals, our packs, our money, the necklace for my wife, the brooch for her sister, the pouches, the statuettes, the herbs, my own special effigies of Adonis and Aphrodite, and the excellent incense sold by Targon near the market place in Amathus: everything.

What was there to do? I had been stupid to trust such obvious rascal in the first place. He had left us not even a sandal to make our journey easier! We walked the remaining four miles to Curium, cursing the thief, the astrologer, ourselves, our feet, and chiefly the rough road which was covered with thorns and horrible pine-needles. Between my bad leg and Phylon's wound it took us six hours. The city is built on a high plateau you see and in the heat it was all we could do to keep going.

Curium is divided into two distinct parts, the Upper and the Lower City. Our first visit had necessarily to be to the proxenos representing Carpasia, a local man named Chariton with business and family connections with our town. He resides in the Upper City near the main square and he was very friendly affording us a loan without the normal precautions of 'proof and identity', for, as it turned out, he had once made a good deal with my father in the days when the old man was still sprightly. In fact he pressed us to stay as his guests, an offer which we were pleased to take up. I had not realised before what a wealthy man he was; but his mansion is magnificent with many spare rooms in a well-kept wing that has its own entrance. This meant we had absolute privacy a luxury indeed. He kept us talking late into the night and we discovered that he was quite a philanthropist and had staged five drama festivals at his own expense. The next day while exploring the town we found a column in the public square commemorating his generosity, though he had not mentioned this in his conversation. He fed and wined us so well that for the second night running we drifted off into a delicious sleep.

Both the upper and lower of Curium posses public squares, broad and well-kept, paved in marble. The palace of the king and the main temple of Apollo Hylates — the patron god of the city — are situated in Upper Curium. The streets otherwise are dark and narrow and only men on foot are allowed through most of them in the day-time. Apparently there have been many fatal accidents involving animals and carts. The temple is a complex and comprises the treasury, the gymnasium and a free lodging house besides the usual sacred edifices. The palace I cannot speak for; it looks well enough from the outside. I was particularly impressed by three buildings: the public baths in Lower Curium which overlook the square and are fitted out with cold, hot and steam baths, two restaurants, three taverns, a games arena and a highly luxurious, though expensive, brothel; an amphitheatre at the south end of the city perched on the edge of a precipice, very pretty and dangerous;

and not far from that, to the West a desolate circular platform of impressive proportions with an altar at the centre.

I went with Chariton to the platform I have just described: Already a large and festive crowd had gathered there bearing the usual religious knick-knacks. Chariton had brought another man with him and as they were chatting about business there was little chance of conversation. Then someone next to me said, 'He is coming!' and I wondered who he meant. I had quite a good view from where I stood, so craned forward to focus on a small knot of men who had entered the central space. They were several youths, three priests and a man who appeared to be bound walked among them, closely attended. For all the world it looked like a public execution or a trial of some sort. The priests stood by the altar praying and the prisoner ascended the platform. I recognised him as the mule driver, the very same scoundrel who had robbed us on the way here! 'Yes', people told me, 'it was Pandorus the murderer (twice over), thief and confidence trickster, who had been captured, tried and sentenced late last night'. 'What are they going to do with him?' I asked, 'I thought this was a religious festival not a place of execution'. 'But it is a religious festival'. I was assured, 'it happens every year; a criminal bearing our sins, is sacrificed to Apollo. It is like expelling poison'.

I found it difficult to watch. After all I knew the man! What if he was the worst of villains—an execution is an execution and not an occasion for rejoicing. The man was forced to run around the perimeter of the area while the youths picked him up and ran out of the arena with him. The crowd too surged forward and there was a general rush down to the cliff-edge. Here Pandorus was swung four or five times in the air before being thrown headfirst to his death in the sea below. Thus ended our mule driver. The theft with which he was charged was not even connected with ours.

Paphos at last! The distance from Curium is not great but the road winds through hills and is extremely steep at times which makes for hard going. As we approached the city we were met by an ever increasing stream of pilgrims, some on foot, some on mule or horseback, converging on the city. Between Paphos and Curium there is a forest of pines where deer wander in large numbers, unafraid and unmolested — the woods of Apollo Hylates. I must just mention this before passing on. The deer are very docile. Two or three came up to us and nudged at our chests in hope of food. Of course we could not resist them. As they are under the protection of Apollo it would be sacrilege to harm them, and we took their solicitations as signs of the god's favour. At two places in the forest streams of clear water issue from the ground and here we rested and refreshed ourselves, and before leaving tossed a coin into the pool, making a wish at the same time. These are the Baths of Aphrodite.

A little later, at roughly the half way mark between the cities, we heard the cry of gulls and came upon a group of islands entirely composed of solid bodies of rock, on which practically every available jut and grag was occupied by some sea-bird, constantly rising and dropping with great shrieks, making it impossible for the eye to follow any single one. There were three other men standing and watching these birds, and discovering that they too were on route for Paphos we fell in with them. The border between Curium and Paphos is marked by a river that flows down from Mount Olympus. This we had to cross, then make a long and tedious ascent before we came to the gentle downhill slope that leads to the sea. This is uninhabited but obviously skilfully irrigated and cultivated indicating that it belonged to the temple of Paphian Aphrodite.

We by-passed Old Paphos and proceeded to the port some sixty stadia distant, for this is the traditional starting point for pilgrims. What a delight this last stage of our journey was: the flat, white rooftops before us reflecting the sunlight before a clear blue sea.

We hurried towards it joyfully. Either side of the road there were sacred trees, imposing in both girth and height, and between them the tended fields stretched away in rich greens and golds. As we approached the town the road became more crowded; mules, donkeys, carts, masters and slaves blocked the road so we had to walk over the fields, but I didn't mind. At the edge of the town, quite unexpectedly, we found ourselves on the brink of a precipice, the base of which was flanked by gigantic rocks. We descended a steep path and there in front of us lay Paphos. Perhaps no place is as beautiful as a man's own home but Paphos opens out to us like a vision.

The first thing to do was to find accommodation, which was no easy task. On our way in we had seen hundreds of people wandering about with poles and makeshift tents, indeed some had already pitched them within a stone's throw of the town itself. Of course Paphos is no metropolis, and on festive occasions the local inhabitants are easily outnumbered by the visitors who come from all parts of the world. Some of the wealthy ones can afford to bribe their way into reserved rooms, others may have friends here with whom they can stay, some may be lucky enough to turn up at inn just as others are moving out, but most people take no chances and bring camping equipment. We were of the third category. We were just drudging dispiritedly down one of the smaller streets when a pair of drunks fell sprawling at our feet, cursing vehemently and tripping up Phylon. A man shouted disparaging comments from a doorway to the effect that he had not let his room to pigs and that such creatures would find more fitting quarters in the sty. We sized up the situation and quickly took up the vacated premises with a little bonus on top of the already rather exorbitant rent, grateful nontheless that our long search had at last yielded some result.

However the crowding problem has another side, which as it turns out is an unusual convenience. Everyday in the appropriate season people arrive and depart, citizens of small villages, inhabitants of foreign towns, pilgrims taking a different route from the one we have chosen—there is therefore no difficulty whatever in getting a letter delivered, for hardly have you stopped to talk to someone when you discover that either he or a friend of his hails from precisely that district to which you desire a message to be sent.

The festival is not due to start for another seven days but there are plenty of things to do. The taverns are full of dancing girls and good wine and if your fancy strays to women you will find numerous houses where you will be delightfully pampered. However a little care ought to be taken, for private establishment are very expensive in season, and you could easily find yourself destitute within a few days. The Temple—girls are less demanding financially, and leave payment to the customer's discretion, though one is expected to contribute something to the unkeep of the temple, and the girls too must live somehow. Of course it is cheaper but there is more to it than mere cost: a temple is after all a temple and one enters in a completely different state of mind.

The Goddess had chosen the temple as her dwelling place: it is she who takes possession of a girl's body when she performs her duties willingly, and indeed I have yet to see brighter, heavier blossom than in the temple gardens of Paphos.

Another way of filling in the time is to hire a guide to take you

64

round town. They tend to be garrulous in the extreme and either bore you with recitations of inaccurate history or, if they think you gullible enough, make up facts with an abandon usually reserved for tumblers and dancing girls of the most audacious sort. Battles, miracles, murders are supposed to have taken place at every street corner. The guides are expensive but if you are lucky you might find a genuine and entertaining man who will make your stay more interesting than it otherwise might have been.

Since arriving here I have had the time to inquire about alternative arrangements for accommodation. There is a temporary shelter provided by the city authorities in a vacant field. This is far from comfortable and is chiefly a desperation measure, at least for people of some substance: the poor of course have no choice. Then there are various clubs that one may 'join' for a price. that provide a floor to sleep on and twenty people to share it with; actors, soldiers, merchants, whatever you declare yourself to be. These are more expensive but hardly more desirable, for they are ideal haunting ground for thieves. As I have always said, one needs luck My landlady is called Tyrranis, a name that fits her well. We managed to obtain the vacant room from her only after a substantial deposit, and that on the excuse that the room had in fact been reserved for a couple of other gentlemen, but that we looked very respectable, as if we could afford a poor woman some security, for after all there were so many shifty characters about who would take advantage of her generosity, and argue about the reasonable rent which was really a piffling sum considering the cleanliness and convenient siting of her house. The formalities of sales-talk are beyond me, for it must have been quite obvious to her that we would take the room at almost any price, but it was impossible to stop her. She would on no account accept foreign money. Would we please go down to the port where we would find the local bankers at their tables, and seek out one Hereidos, a particular friend of hers who would charge us only 5% rather than the customary 6% for changing our currency. I sent Phylon down to do this. While he was away she plied me with offers of girls and boys at cut-throat prices, but I kept assuring her, with moderate success, that the only thing I was presently interested in was a place to lay my head, a privilege for which she could consider herself as good as paid. To do her justice the house is comparatively clean but she must make a fortune, for it is a large house and most of the guests, including ourselves sleep above the stables of which there are ten, arranged in a semi-circle round the yard. We reach our room by way of a long balcony that runs the length of the compound, a set of stairs at either end. My room is not intended for 'stay-at-home' guests: its furniture consists of a solitary bed.

The social life of the city revolves round clubs and every person in the area belongs to one or other of them. They remain open day and night and are full of conversation; gossip, information, abstract argument, trade deals; offseason they are really professional associations but boundaries blur at this time. Their chosen representatives sit on the City Council, which in turn, advises the King. Actors, potters, builders, even slaves have their appropriate clubs—Phylon has in fact joined this last and has made some useful contacts—but there are also those with a merely social function where common attitudes rather than common livelihoods form the basis. There is a Literary Association, a Ladies Circle, a travellers club, and anyone may join these for an annual subscription which covers funeral expenses and a memorial tablet when a member dies. Most of the clubs maintain their own burial chamber,—quite palatial affairs some of them—where members are interred. One can trace back generations of builders and fish-merchants in gaunt subterranean halls, guarded by Doric columns, accessible through silent quadrangles. The oldest tombs belong to the Phoenicians of the city who started to custom.

Phylon attended a festival called Hierodouli, which is celebrated by the local slaves. He had heard about it down at his club and described the proposed proceedings with great enthusiasm so that in all fairness I felt it would be wrong of me to refuse him permission. He really is a very good man, the best slave I have ever had, and highly intelligent.

The Hierodouli, he explained, always takes place a week before the Aphrodisia proper, and is a few days in preparation. Branches of the myrtle tree are used to build huts, and inside these huts are placed the usual stone and wax figures of the goddess, upon a bed of soft grass or other greenery. Honours are paid to an ivory statue of Aphrodite, which is credited with magical powers and has symbolic associations with the story of Myrrha and her transformation, as well as with Pygmalion's statue, that lived and walked by the goddess's aid. The slaves garland themselves with flowers and take their places in the huts trusting that the ritual would benefit their powers of procreation. Many have visions or go into trances. They say that apparitions of their free ancestors and their far away countries sometimes appear. As for the efficacy of the rites, Phylon is childless, so I earnestly join in his prayer.

66

Paphos possesses only one amphitheatre but it can seat up to 30,000 people, today, being the first day of the Festival Plays, all the seats were taken. During the festival there are continual performances everyday from early afternoon to late in the evening, and a panel of judges award prizes to the finest authors and actors of each particular day. On the evidence of this afternoon's entertainment I would say the standard falls somewhat short of the best, but in their rude simplicity the plays can be very moving if a little declamatory. Mostly these are tragedies; chance and human folly are the directing forces, few however are moral or speculative in any challenging way: The statement is made, the consequences follow and one does not question the characters' motives or the assumptions of the plot. Some have happy endings like the prize winning performance I attended. It was called CINYRAS and showed how the Paphian Priest-King dealt quite successfully with conflicting moral and religious principles at the time of the Trojan War. (The plot went as follows: Ulysses arrives at Paphos with a Greek force and requests Cinyras's aid in the proposed Trojan expedition. Cinyras cannot refuse because the Greek forces are overwhelming, so swears to tribute forty ships. The Greeks leave and Cinyras is left to ponder on his dire situation, for as High Priest of Aphrodite he may not provide forces for the destruction of Troy, the side favoured by the Goddess, nor, on the other hand may he break his solemn promise for fear of devine vengeance. Being a pragmatist he hits upon the ingenious solution of sending but one ship, with thirty-nine small scale models on board. This is despatched to Agamemnon, the commander in chief of the Greek forces, thus absolving himself of his oath, while avoiding the offence to Aphrodite. As a palliative he encloses a magnificent breast-plate for Agamemnon to wear—the very breast-plate described by Homer in the Iliad. The moral? In this world you must have your wits about you!

How crowded Paphos has become! I thought the place was more than full when I first arrived but now there is barely room to move. Greeks, Egyptians, Persians, Ethiopians, jostle in the streets and all I hear are foreign voices and the cries of tradesmen. Some brothels are shutting their doors and allowing in only regulars, or those who look particularly rich or important. The temples are popular of course as is the museum. I was there this morning but could hardly see the exhibits. It is housed within the main temple enclosure and contains many objects of veneration: sculptures of gods and heroes, paintings, armour, spoils of war and other historical fragments. What do I recall? There

67

was Pygmalion's Galatea statue, the hide and tusks of the boar that killed Adonis, and the robe and lyre of Cinyras, the lyre with which he outplayed Apollo in a contest. The sword of Teucer is also here among other Homeric relics; the golden apple with which Paris, by awarding it to Aphrodite rather than Athene or Hera, effectively commenced the Trojan War, and the box given by Phylis to her unfaithful husband Demophon which drove him mad as soon as he opended it. All these things are here arranged in hierarchies of local interest: I caught a glimpse of most of them ...

The Aphrodisia begins on the sea front—the very place where Aphrodite first touched land, marked now by her favourite shrine: two large conical stones propped against each other, forming an arch surmounted by a carved dove, and sheltering a statue of the goddess gazing out over the sea. This statue set on a plinth while, on either side of the arch stands a column, heavy footed, like sentinels the pair. The arch I must explain is no artifice but a natural wonder such as nature often throws together by chance or hidden design (like the tree outside Carpasia in the shape of an old woman with sagging breasts) and the image looks more perfect within it than it might have in a more ordered structure—she looks the goddess herself.

First came the Oiling. We stood in prayer, while a Priestess rubbed the statue all over with fine oil, then she wiped it off. The virgins came forward, young girls just into puberty, and washed their naked bodies in the waves. Then they danced a short time caressing all the while an effigy of the goddess, which they passed among themselves. The nature of this dance is purely sensual and provides initation into the arts of seduction and sensual life. The priest signals the end of the dance with a gesture to welcome the arrival of Autumn, the time for the gathering of fruits, and the girls disperse, seeking lovers among the crowd. Then the priest led us down to the main temple, a long walk through the extensive Sacred Gardens. The path before and after this was lined by street-vendors selling incense and small effigies of the goddess. They did a roaring trade and on the way up I saw several vacated stalls, presumably because their occupants had sold out all their stock. Yet often just as one man would be packing up, a second would arrive with a fresh lot to take over his pitch. I bought some incense and a couple of figurines.

As soon as we arrived at the temple we were offered refreshment and invited to look around. I knew something of its history already, having paid close attention to a series of paintings in the museum which showed the building at different stages. At one time it used to be a modest structure, neither big nor particularly ornate, built by King Cinyras on the site of an older temple which had been dedicated to a goddess known as the Great Mother, but as its fame grew and spread over the whole world, and the pilgrims gathered with their wealth and piety to consult the resident cracle, it increased in size and splendour until few temples in the world could vie with it. Thus it is today. In front of the great gate (a little away removed from it) stand two pylons wreathed in pomegranates and surmounted by doves. Behind these a line of rose bushes defines a semi-circular enclosure at the centre of which is an altar. The gate itself is decorated with reliefs of soldiers, hunters and priests, and two tall towers, joined together at three quarters of their height by three adjoining chambers with windows, stand either side of it. On the flat roof of the chambers are displayed the emblems of Aphrodite—the crescent moon and a star. Past the gate a covered collonade extends to a black statue of the goddess, which is itself exposed to the weather, though tradition proclaims that no rain has ever fallen on it. The outside walls of the temple are built of bricks and the roofs made of clay. The sacred enclosure is large and contains the main temple, numerous sacred trees and the living quarters of its various officials, both priests and priestesses. There is a treasury, a storehouse of all the marvellous donations made by wealthier visitors and also of various records and spoils of war in an underground chamber. But I must not forget a more natural yet no less special attraction, Aphrodite's harbingers, the sacred doves that depart in the early summer but always reappear in time for the great festival. These doves are reputed to accompany the goddess on her annual visit to Lybia: their safe return is a sign of Aphrodite's presence in Paphos—also of her approval and participation.

So much for the temple. The next three days were taken up by sacrifices, prayers, singing and dancing competitions, readings of poetry, athletics, love feasts in the woods around the temple—in fact such a turmoil of activity that I cannot claim to have it properly in perspective. The sacrifices are the most impressive: these usually take place in the morning, at first light, and set the tone for the rest of the day. Of course we had all seen sacrifices before but never such pomp, precision or significance.

As a fully paid up member of the Actors Club I was entitled to participate in any of the performing arts, though of course this was not expected of one who had only the previous week joined and was likely to leave within the following week. I did perform however and this is how it came about. A day before the Aphrodisia got under way I visited the club and was drawn into a conversation concerning the relative merits of various metrical schemes in religious poetry and I found myself taking the side of one of the local experts who was both actor and poet. We agreed on everything so wholeheartedly that we left the company and decided to toast each other's health the rest of the evening. It turned out that he was indeed to read one of his latest works, specially composed for the Aphrodisia, and he recited it to me, some three or four times with different intonations, asking my opinion on the effectiveness of each. We tried it one way then the other, analysed it, declaimed it, whispered it, until I knew it almost as well as he did himself. We drank until late into the night then went home our defferent ways. It was the next morning a boy tapped at my door with a message from my new friend that I was to follow his son round to their house as urgently as possible. I did so and it turned out that the poet on his way home last night had fallen down and broken some ribs, and was now confined to his room. Would I be kind enough, he beseeched me, to learn his verses and perform them in his place the day after the next? We were so much in sympathy, he assured me that I was certain to give a moving performance and win a prize. So I became the focus of attention in the temple grounds one night. It is a pity to ruin such a happy story by admitting that I won no prize and thus disappointed my friend, but honesty compels me to own that I shall never rival the professional readers in dramatic and visual presentation (though I have a sneaking conviction that my performance was more truly felt and correctly interpreted than most of the winning ones). It was very exciting nevertheless and perhaps now I shall have alternative occupation in my old age.

There is so much to say about the Aphrodisia that I cannot include everything. There is so much free food that I have doubts whether I will be recognized when I get home: my belly is swollen and my cheeks are red, unusual sights!

The Aphrodisia is the central event at this time, but coincident with and relating obliquely to it are the Mysteries of the Cinyraids which also attract many visitors. I myself was unable to attend the greater part of these rites, though I had plenty of opportunity to witness the four days of preparation and trial that any would-be initiate must undergo: many fall by the wayside here and one may be excluded for any defect in character, which means of course that most people with a grain of conscience will think twice about attempting it. Mind you

I have seen the unceremonius desmissal of a fellow who was discovered to have a criminal record. Really this is for higher adepts, those who will enter into a close and mysterious communication with the Goddess.

As to what happens, on the first day there is a fixed rota of strenuous physical competitions, running, wrestling and gymnastics. Not all candidates are equally fit and it is a pathetic though not uncomical sight to see some ludicrous figure attempt headstands, somersaults and such.

The second day is devoted mainly to sea-bathing, but I missed this owing to other commitments.

The third day calls for less exertion, and consists of devotional exercises and oblation chiefly the ceremonial offering of wine and fruit and flowers. There were half the candidates left by this stage. Those who had survived so far then spent the last day fasting and in constant prayer which eliminated a few more. The hardy few then paid the necessary fee to the high priest and received in return a lump of salt and a stone phallus (salt being emblematic of the sea, Aphrodite's birthplace, and the phallus of creativity). Thus abandoning the life of the senses, as symbolized by the money, and assuming a more spiritual existence. Even so, before being admitted into the temple the novices are made to take another vow of purity and must bathe in holy water. And these are only the preliminary stages—the initiation now begins in earnest. Needless to say I would know nothing of the following had it not been for information given to me by an acquaintance who had got so far once but was terribly disappointed to succumb to a fever which prevented him from completing the course.

According to him the first advanced stage is the reading of the mysteries by a priest Questions are then asked in a cryptic form and these had to be correctly answered. My acquaintance did so but refuses to elaborate on the nature of the mysteries or of the questions—I naturally did not press him. Next they are offered pancakes and honey and are declared mystics. I almost forgot to add that they wear certain magical garments during this last ceremony, the total effect of which is to repel evil. It was at this point that my informant contracted fever. He hung on desperately for the first day of the second stage but will say very little about it save that it lasted two days and he took part in some unspecified rituals connected with the myth of Adonis.

Neither he, nor anyone else knows anything of the third and final stage save that there is one such, but men of course make vulgar guesses at sadistic and orgiastic forms. It may safely be assumed that the ex-

71

periences are ecstatic, one theory being that emblems of the goddess are employed in some way.

One man asserts that an obelisk is used as well as the sacred doves. This ecstasy would be a kind of divine madness and the sign of possession by the holy spirit.

I have decided to stay in Paphos for a while. In a few weeks time most of the foreign pilgrims will have gone and I will be able to wander round town at a leisurely pace. The sea will be choppy next month- they must go soon. Besides, then I will be able to seak fresh accommodation: this Tyrranis woman is quite unbearable. If it's not, 'Make sure your feet are clean before treading on my floor!' it is 'Let me introduce you to my cousin. She is a virgin, young, but so clever, you would not believe the things she can do!' Indeed she is right. 1 cannot believe what she says at the best of times.

But it is fruitless complaining—I shall continue dreaming of a decent comfortable room in civilised company. I shall probably be home before the Adonia if all goes well.

Gradually the fact dawns on me that I shall soon be home. I have not mentioned the times when I have felt utterly wretched and homesick. But it is always sad to come to the end of something, especially of a project one has been planning for years. I shall miss the element of risk, that pleasantly intoxicating feeling of having neither duty nor home to draw me into regular ways.

Here in Marium they have just finished celebrating their version of the Adonia festival. The Adonia! you will say, surely this is out of season! The locals however staunchly defend this practice and assert that other towns have their calendars wrong and they adduce this and that as proof. In fact they concentrate on a different aspect of the legend so it is not as ridiculous as it might appear. For them Autumn is the sterile season and Winter a welcome change towards fecundity. Indeed they enjoy mild and pleasant winters.

Before going on to describe their procedures, I will say something about my last few weeks at Paphos. I did manage to find new lodgings but only after a very nasty scene with the inn-keeper Tyrranis, who presented me with a vastly inflated bill, and tried to cajole me into staying according to the rules of some contract which I had never set eyes on. What screaming there was and what stabbing of fingers! Phylon and I eventually just pushed her out of the way and left her threatening dire forms of vengeance. I hope never to meet such a monster again. But the rest of the time was most restful: slowly the town emptied, and the pace of life slowed down to a gentle stroll. Phylon and I frequented our respective clubs and my poet friend recovered and forgave me for letting him down in the competition. We went drinking and walking along the sea at evening, paid regular visits to the temple and the museum and I struck up a relationship with our new landlord who was guite glad to let a vacant room. And so the days drifted on and grew colder and I almost forgot the purpose of my visit until one day it came to me that the Marium Adonia was almost on us. We sadly packed and bid farewell to all our recent acquaintances, promising to return, to maintain contact and so forth, and left. I don't know when I will return for one cannot do this sort of thing regularly, but perhaps, having made some useful contacts here, I will have a pretext.

After Paphos, Marium seems rather insignificant, and I cannot bring myself to give a legthy description of its ordinary streets and humbler temples. This is a little unfair to the town I suppose but I will take a few paragraphs to deal with the Adonia itself.

The first day was one of mourning for the death of Adonis, and we ate only green vegetables; the women chewed garlic in order to repel the men's advances for both wine and copulation are forbidden. The purification began at dawn: prayers were chanted, the walls and doors of the temple smeared with myrtle resin, and a lamb was sacrificed. This last is an act of excorcism; the creature is flayed and its hide used to mop up the blood which has spurted across the temple floor. One is forbidden to touch its flesh for that is where the exorcised spirits are supposed to take refuge.

The women brought flowers and aromatic shrubs and placed them on a bier inside the temple; while this was going on others were casting live doves onto a pyre in a specially constructed oven made to contain two seperate fires, so that as the doves flew out of one they blundered into the other and were thus consumed. It is a pitiful sound but also a very exciting one to hear the flapping of wings and the cries of the birds above the roaring fire, up and down up and down, then falling silent. It is amazing how closely one identifies oneself with them: somehow they strike an echo in the spirit. Once upon a time they used to put people in

73

there. The idea is to impersonate the death and resurrection of the devine Adonis.

After this we returned to our houses and lodgings and prepared a small shrine using stone images of Adonis. These are placed at the entrances and surrounded by fruits and vegetables and cakes baked into phallic shapes. Every house in the town sported such a display. Then in the evening comes the central event, the Gardens of Adonis. The 'Gardens' themselves are no more than a miscellaneous collection of gold and silver containers which are filled with fast-growing decorative plants, no more than eight days old some of them but the whole makes an impressive show, especially in the evening light which as it catches the precious metal gives it a dull glow. The women bear these, along with the Adonis figures, in a dark parade through the streets, weeping and wailing for the dead hero. Their breasts are bared and those who are not actually carrying anything beat themselves there in time with the lamentations.

I would rather face any number of savages than five or six crazed women. There have been times when the women have become quite frenzied, and the city authorities thought it necessary to lay down strict guidelines as to the conduct of this demonstration. The procession in fact wound its way down to the sea without any violent outbreaks, where the Gardens were cast, to the accompaniment of wild prayers and even wilder songs, far out into the waves.

Later the fast was broken with a meal of pork. In this detail too the Marians vary from the rest of mankind. The rest of us would never dream of touching pork during the Adonia for we associate it with the boar not with his victim, but here it is quite the other way about and Adonis is assumed to be incarnate in the pig; hence the sacrifice and devouring of the beast seems to them perfectly in order. I must say I had more qualms about this than almost any other divergence from normal custom, but I did eventually eat of it. I had to examine my conscience very deeply to ensure that it was not only hunger from the prolonged fast that persuaded me to touch the stuff. When the meal is ended the fat and bones are burned as a sacrifice on the altar.

On the second day the mood was far more joyful. Flowers were cast into the sea and we celebrated the resurrection of Adonis. There were animal sacrifices, feasting and mating: Aphrodite was reunited with her lover. A marriage ceremony was enacted between the High Priest, representing Adonis, and one of the priestesses who had previously been chosen to take the part of the goddess. This was accompanied by much music and praying, and the witnesses sprinkled corn, figs and dry nuts over the couple's heads and round their feet. Meanwhile a room was prepared, strewn with flowers and decorated with all kinds of vegetation, where the pair immediately consummated their marriage. Of course we were not present and the area of the temple where the chamber was located was sealed off, but the union is widely proclaimed through the town and people rejoice for they believe that fertility is bestowed upon their lands by this act.

By this time it had grown late and the people dispersed, bringing the festival to a close. I wandered back to my lodgings on the outskirts of town, thinking already of my homeward journey. Often during the last few days my thoughts have returned to Paphos, and I have been strongly tempted to retrace my steps and spend a few more weeks there. But these things are impossible: one can no more cast off the ties of normal life than the colour of one's hair. However I shall certainly make a point of visiting Paphos again. I have a little money in my purse, which will do to pay off my landlord and buy some food for the journey.

CHAPTER FOUR

SURVIVING INFLUENCES OF THE CULT OF APHRODITE IN CYPRUS

To this day, Aphrodite has not entirely ceased to be part of the religion of the Cypriot people. We have already mentioned how the black stone of the goddess, built into the wall of a church, was until recently venerated by Cypriot women who believed in its power to cure sterility. We may find many other examples of this kind of folk custom. In the district of Paphos there exist the ruins of an orthodox church dedicated to Our Lady Aphroditissa (The Venus Mary). Another church, in the same district is called Our Lady Galatariotissa, whose name derives from Galatea, the wife of Pygmalion. The Virgin Mary represented in this church has the power to cure mothers who have lost their ability to produce milk for their babies. Even the girdle of Aphrodite, famous for its power to enslave the hearts of men, is still in existence and in use in the monastery of Trooditissa: It is now called the belt of the Blessed Virgin Mary and is lent out to Christian ladies who wish to become pregnant. The monastery of Chrysoroyiatissa, on the same mountain range, translated freely means Our Lady of the Golden Breasts, but some people claim that the name derives from the hill on which it stands and looks like a female breast. Visitors to both these monasteries who desire a cure offer the Queen of Heaven wax models showing the afflicted part of the body just as they would have done for Aphrodite.

Engaged couples, and lovers in general, visit St George of the Island who is particularly understanding of their problems. Young men go to him to pray that they may be given the girl of their choice. His church is in the district of Paphos overlooking the seashore, opposite a little uninhabited island, and his ikon represents him as a handsome, virile youth, not unlike Adonis.

Again if one walks from Ktima to Old Paphos one makes the startling discovery that Aphrodite's old companions Eros and Anteros have become Christian saints. Two shrines belonging to St Eros and St Anteros are carved into the rocks and both contain a small altar on which visitors may light cadles or dedicate strips of clothing. The functions of the two saints are similar to those of their ancient counterparts, namely one creates feelings of love and the other either punishes those who fail to respond to love or terminates romantic associations he considers to be improper. There are two ways to procure the assistance of these two saints, one either donates to them a piece of clothing belonging to the person whose affections one wishes to influence or one takes a sample of soil from the shrine and scatters it over the person one loves. The saints seem to use these items to identify their target. There is an element of risk involved in using this venue to gain somebody's affection, for few people can now tell with certainty which shrine belongs to which saint, and as we know the two divinities performed opposite functions. While I was examining these shrines, I was approached by an old lady and was advised by her to return to the spot at sunset and to stand at the correct distance from the rocks. I was now to watch for the appearance of a shadow like that of a pig on one of the shrines that would belong to St Anteros.

The pig is of course an animal connected with the cult of Aphrodite. It was a boar that killed Adonis, and even now no pork is eaten at wedding feasts for fear that the bride might become widow. These wedding feasts last for three days, like the Aphrodisia festival celebrating the union of the goddess with her lover Adonis. After the church ceremony it is customary in some villages to offer the bridegroom a pomigranate (sacred to Aphrodite) which he then cracks on the door of the wedding chamber. In other villages the bridegroom is required to kill a cockerel (sacred to Eros) and spray the blood onto the doorstep of the wedding chamber. Both events are types of sacrifice belonging more to ancient traditions than Christian culture.

One rather illogical compromise between the cult of Aphrodite and Cypriot Christianity is the belief of modern Cypriots that only women are capable of committing sexual sins. This explains the comparative modesty of Cypriot women which contrasts strongly with the excesses of the men. Unlike their ancestors Cypriot men demand that their wives be virgins on their wedding day and deflowering a virgin is considered by these as the ultimate satisfaction. This ambivalent attitude has had some tragic results, leading in some cases to murder.

One of the best known festivals of Cyprus takes place on Whit-

Sunday and its origins seem to be rooted in the Aphrodisia. This is held in all coastal towns and includes competitions of song, dance, swimming and diving. The Orthodox Church has done its best to present it in a Christian light by calling it the Kataclysmos (the Deluge and Noah's Rescue) but there is little doubt that the Cypriots who flock to the nearest shore to splash each other with water and enjoy themselves are unconsiously partaking in a rather more pagan rite.

Ten miles west of Larnaca (the site of ancient Citium) is a conical mountain, famous for the monastery of Stavrovouni, which perches precariously at its summit. In ancient times and for a thousand years before the birth of Jesus, on this same spot stood the temple of Aphrodite Akrea where the Cypriots went to pray for rain. The story of Stavrovouni is worth relating because the functions and character of the two religious institutions which have shared it resemble each other to a remarkable degree.

After a long drought that lasted for ten years and almost depopulated the island, St Helena arrived in Cyprus carrying with her the Cross of Christ which she found in Jerusalem. Soon after her arrival the rain began to fall bringing new life to the land. The river at the bottom of Stavrovouni began to flow again and the grateful people renamed it the Queen's River for Helena was the queen mother of Byzantium. One night Helena slept by the riverside and when she woke in the morning she found to her great distress that the Holy Cross had disappeared from her tent. After a long search it was found on the mountain of Aphrodite where the goddess of love had her temple, so St Helena took it as a sign that she should build a monastery there. This she did and deposited in it part of the true cross renaming the mountain Stavrovouni (The Mount Of The Holy Cross). Over the years countless miracles of healing and rainmaking have been performed by the monks with the assistance of the cross.

Legend has it that Stavrovouni was built using the forced labour of a horde of devils, a myth readily accepted by anyone who is acquainted with the topography of the place. Certainly it would have needed pretty devilish work to have approached such an awkward site. Apparently Helena conscripted 40 demons as masons, and when their work was finished she enticed them down a deep well, ostensibly for the purpose of fetching water. However when they were all in she took the opportunity of sealing up the well. Like Aphrodite Apaturia, St Helena was capable of deception. The ruins of the pagan temple are still visible at the south-east corner of the monastery.

Some trees on the mountain of Stavrovouni are held to be as sacred as their predecessors in pagan times, notably an old pine tree which has assumed a biomorphic aspect and appear to be kneeling as though at prayer. This tree has a cross nailed to its bent trunk and is offered food, drinks and prayers by pilgrims who believe that it has bent over in reverence of Helena as she passed by. Other people believe that the pine was orignally exceedingly proud and had ignored the saint, who then retaliated by blasting it with a thunderbolt which caused it to repent and kneel. Tree-worship survives in many parts of Cyprus. Miraculous trees which are believed to cure diseases are usually found near tombs of saints and are always covered with rags of clothing and human hair hung by devotees on their branches. The most famous of these sacred trees is that of St Solomoni in Paphos.

South west of Stavrovouni, on a hill between the Turkish villages of Aplanta and Kivisili is a strange shrine dedicated to St Black, a lady saint. Like Aphrodite's companions Delight, Fulfilment, and others, St Black has no distinct personality and she probably derived her name from the black stones which abound around her cave. This saint is another miracle worker specialising in procreative effects and those who wish to enlist her assistance must offer to her a strip torn from their clothing. The bushes around the shrine are covered with colourful pieces of cloth hanging from the branches like flags.

There are other sacred caves, some of which are associated with springs and wells. The best known is found outside Famagusta and is believed to be the tomb of St Barnabas. Its entrance is shadowed by eucalyptus trees. A flight of steps leads to an underground chamber, at the far end of which is a deep well of holy water. The remains of the saint are not present because they had been removed to Constantinople during the reign of Emperor Zeno in the fifth century, but pilgrims from all over the island still visit the tomb to fetch holy water for their sick. The entrance to the cave is decorated with pieces of clothing left by people who have been cured.

From these examples it is evident that a kind of polytheism survives. It is true that the church hierarchy does not approve of the worshipping of saints but at the village level priests and their parishioners believe in specialised spirits, who are semi divine and who can help them in specific situations. Thus St Therapon is appealed to in case of stomach-ache, St Kyrillos for indigestion, St Kyriakos for ear-ache and St Anna to ease the pains of childbirth. There are also the venerable protectors of sailors, drivers, pedestrians and other travellers. The remarkable St Mnason, the Cypriot saint mentioned in the New Testament, is the protector of tax dodgers. St Paul would have been quite horrified by some of these practices but the church leaders justify them on the grounds that saints have the power to intercede with God. Saints are bribed in exactly the same way as Aphrodite was in order to gain their favours. The churches of miracle-working saints are extravagantly decorated with presents of gold and silver ornaments and in many farmlands there are sacred trees given to saints for their services to the farmers' families.

The sanctity of relics, familiar to votaries of Aphrodite, is still upheld by Cyptiots who believe in the magical properties of certain ikons, the remains of saints and any object associated with them.

Adonis and Aphrodite had exercised a powerful influence on the imagination of the ancient Cypriots and it is not difficult to find correspondences between these two figures and those of Jesus and the Virgin As in the case of Aphrodite, Mary's festivals, legends and emblems vary greatly from one place of worship to another, so that to a stranger it might seem that many different divinities are being worshipped rather than one. Mary's epithets are as numerous as those of Aphrodite— Madonna of Kykkou, Chrysopolitissa, Sotera etc—and her designation as the Queen of the Universe is similar to Aphrodite's title, the Queen of Heaven. Jesus and Adonis were both perfect, died violently and were resurrected.

Legends relating to Mary and her miraculous deeds are still being invented and told in many versions. Some of these tales are variations on stories about Aphrodite, and their narration usually begins with, "It is said..." Thus: "It is said that the anemone sprang from the blood of the Virgin Mary, who wounded her feet while wandering about the country side looking for Jesus after he had been crucified" Many other flowers are supposed to have sprung from the tears she shed when told of her son's death.

There are numerous similarities between the worship of Jesus and of Adonis. Both Gods are considered incarnate in the instruments of their death; the cross being venerated by Christians as deeply as the swine was by the votaries of Adonis. Moreover, Jesus, like Adonis, is sacrificed to himself and fed to his worshippers in the mystery of Holy Communion. Trees figure prominently in both their cults, the olive tree being as sacred to the modern Cypriot as was the myrtle tree to his ancestors. It is believed that people who sleep under olive trees will

80

enjoy pleasant dreams, for the olive has power against evil spirits. The oil of the olive is indispensible to Orthodox Christian ritual—the resin of the Myrtle was necessary to Adonian rites. The Cypriots celebrate an Olive Sunday during which, branches of the olive tree are taken into churches to be consecrated for use as incense. These branches remain in the church for forty days and are then taken home by their owners who burn them when occasion demands, in portable incense burners, to exorcise evil spirits from the house or to fend off the evil eye. On New Year's Day, fresh leaves of the olive tree are thrown onto wood fires by girls and boys who chant all the while a three verse poem in which they entreat St Basil to tell them whether or not their sweethearts are true. The fresh leaves usually leap out of the fire and the length of the leap indicates the depth of a lovers feeling. The myrtle tree has not been entirely replaced by the olive for it is still used in churches at festival times, and the coaches that take village pilgrims to religious festivals are always decorated with its branches.

But the greatest festival on the church calendar is Easter, and here one may find further correspondence between the old Adonia rites and the present Christian form. Immediately before the festival begins there is a period of fasting. Now as in old days, this is accompanied by abstinence from sexual intercourse. Then there is the preparation of paximadia, bread rolls and cakes of phallic shape which are made by all village housewives so that they may be eaten over Easter. Such cakes appear frequently in pre-Christian Cypriot ritual. They are mentioned in certain places as offerings to Adonis and Aphrodite, being broken up into small pieces and placed in containers round statues of Adonis. At sacrifice ceremonies when the victim was brought to the altar pieces of bread cake were sprinkled over its head. Special wedding cakes were eaten by the bride and groom at marriage ceremonies and many nature spirits, associated with Aphrodite, were offered similar cakes made of flour, oil and honey. The phallic cakes prepared by modern Cypriot housewives are not all consumed by members of the family. Some of them are given to domestic animals and on the night of January 5th, specially made cakes dipped in honey, are thrown onto the roofs of the houses to be consumed by a fantastic breed of hideous but friendly spirits known as the Kalikantzari.

On Good Friday, young women collect aromatic flowers with which they decorate the local church and use what is left to make a pile for the funeral bier representing the body of Jesus. In the evening of the same day, the bier with its load of flowers is carried through the streets in procession so that the faithful may bid farewell to their dead God. This terminates at the church where it started and the flowers are distributed by the priest among the congregation. On the following day there is another church service, ending at midnight when the resurrection of Christ is proclaimed by the priest. The joyous message is given in the phrase "Christ is Risen" and at its utterance, the people light candles, wish happiness to each other, ring church bells, explode fireworks... Branches of the Myrtle tree are scattered about the floor of the church by the priest. After these ceremonies people return home and as soon as they arrive they greet the plants in their gardens with the phrase "Christ is Risen, plant" thus informing them of the arrival of spring. Then they commence preparations for the Easter feast. Men kill the animals and skin them, the women chop the meat up and cook it, so that by early morning the atmosphere is filled with the sweet smell of spring lamb, roasted on wood fires.

CHAPTER FIVE

THE STORY OF CYPRUS

THE GREEKS SETTLE IN CYPRUS

Following the settlement of the Mycenaeans, and shortly after twelve hundred years BC, there arrived in Cyprus the first of the Grecian settlers, their appearance heralded by the conclusion of the Trojan War. These friendly invaders soon made their mark. Many heroes of the Trojan excursion indelibly stamped their memory on the history of Cyprus in the names they gave to the towns that so many of them founded.

Teucer founded Salamis, Chalcanor founded Idalion, Alexandrus founded Lapethos and Chytrus gave his name to Chytri. Akamas, not satisfied with naming a town, named a whole area—that of the northwest corner of Cyprus in which are the famous Baths of Aphrodite. Another, Agapenor, settled in the Kingdom of Cinyras in Paphos and founded the town of New Paphos.

Not every noble Grecian soldier who strayed upon the shores of Cyprus stayed, however, and some, the victims of storms and shipwrecks, obviously homesick, and weary of foreign lands, no matter how lovely, left almost as soon as they had come, leaving no sign of their presence. They left for Greece, or perhaps some other fate, for in those cruel times, no man was master of his destiny. Not even great heroes, nor even great Kings, not even Menelaus himself, King of Sparta, or even his notorious wife, Helen, for whom the ten year war with Troy was waged. Not even Demophon, hero of the Trojan seige, friend of Menelaus, and himself Prince of Athens.

Demophon had fought hard and long in this fierce and legendary war, and, out of the necessity for a hard-earned rest rather than out of love, so it seems, he courted and successfully seduced the beautiful Thracian princess Phyllis, with whom he lived for a while after the war had ended. Phyllis thought her Champion was the most beautiful

83

man on the earth, and she showered him with her soft warm love every minute of every day. Demophon, however, after a few blissful months, grew bored, and, the warrior spirit in him, the wanderer, now refreshed, grew restless, and daily, this longing to be a soldier again, this lust for fresh adventure grew.

With that typical lack of courage that great soldiers often experience in the face of the unpredicatable; for instance, a potentially angry woman, Demophon, instead of nobly facing his lover and revealling to her the sad truth of his feelings, decides to slyly sneak away. He tells Phyllis what men have said for centuries, that he has 'urgent business' to attend to in Athens immediately, and must leave right away, but promises to return after a month.

Phyllis is no fool, and by means of a parting gift, she gives her champion a beautiful jewelled box, and tells him that he must never open this box unless, after the month has passed, he has decided never to return.

Happy to be free again, Demophon takes to the open sea, and heads for Athens, but no sooner have they set their sails, when a great storm blows them off their course, and forces them to land at Cyprus, where Menelaus and Helen are staying at that time.

One morning, as the same sun that had set over Troy not four months before was beginning to rise, overcome by curiosity, Demophon decides to open the jewelled casket that Phyllis had given him. Sighing perhaps, at the skill with which he had escaped from the horrors of permanent domesticity, the Prince of Athens slowly opened the box and looked inside.

What he saw filled him with such terror as he had never known, and screaming, insane with fear, he climbed upon his brave war-horse for the last time and rode into the sea that had saved him from a love that had died, and that same sea claimed his life.

King Menelaus sat alone in his room and wondered what could have driven his friend to end his life in such a fashion, but he was never to know, and neither shall we ever know, for the terrible secret of that lovers' parting gift was buried by Menelaus with his friend, in the soil of Cyprus, and will lie forever with the secrets of the earth.

Not long after this, Menelaus and Helen returned to Sparta, and were never again visitors to that land.

ASSYRIANS, EGYPTIANS AND PERSIANS

A GOLDEN AGE FOR CYPRIOT SCULPTURE

The Assyrian occupation of Cyprus ended at the end of the eighth century BC., after which the island passed successively through the hands of a number of conquerors. In 560BC Cyprus was occupied by the Egyptian King Amasis who forced the Cypriot kings to become his vassals and pay him an annual tribute. In 540BC the island was conquered by Cyrus the Elder, the founder of the Persian Empire.

Under the occupation, the Cypriot rulers were allowed to keep their royal status and a large measure of autonomy. All they were asked to do, was to pay tribute to their conquerors, and issue them with ships and armies whenever the occasion demanded. Apart from this they were allowed to rule their subjects as they wished, issue their own coins, and even sign treaties with foreign kings. These priveledges were partly due to the fact that Cyprus was the centre of the cult of Aphrodite, a goddess venerated throughout the whole of the Middle East, and, subsequently, as a religious centre was treated less harshly by its conquerors; this situation allowed the development of a native culture which gave birth to the Cyprus School of sculpture.

Cypriot sculpture was influenced by the art of the three great civilisations of Eastern Europe and the Middle East: the Greek, Egyptian and Assyrian, and one of its main characteristics is the way in which it incorporates stylistic elements and ideas from these sources. These influences were inevitable because of the geographical and political situation of the island, but in spite of them Cypriot sculpture developed into a creative and original school. Cypriot sculptors seemed to have been less inhibited than their colleagues in neighbouring countries from religious and stylistic conventions and they developed a semi-realistic form of expression that reminds us of twentieth century art. Their subject matter, in many examples, is concerned with human beings in their every day lives. Soldiers, artisans and nobles, are represented in a way that indicates their occupations, their social rank (in group compositions), their preference for fashion, even their personal characteristics. Some Cypriot statues of pre-classical times look like portraits.

A major achievement of Cypriot sculpture was that it gave art one of its eternal subjects, Hercules the Lionslayer, whose story was exploited by sculptors of the ancient world for many centuries. The original Lionslayer used to adorn one of the squares of the Cypriot town Amathus. The statue stood 14 feet high and showed the famous hero Hercules holding a dead lioness by her hind legs, her forepaws touching the ground. The statue was dug up by archaeologists in 1873 and was transferred to Constantinople where it acquired notoriety as an object of ugliness and barbarity. The sculpture, in fact, is a work of great skill, but in the age of impressionism and art nouveau European intellectuals were unable to recognise beauty in a dynamic structure like the Colossus of Amathus.

It is difficult to say if Cypriot sculpture had an influence on the sculpture of Assyria and Egypt but we can be certain that it influenced Greek sculpture profoundly. Cypriot statues have been found in many parts of Greece, taken there as souvenirs by pilgrims who visited the shrines of Aphrodite in their thousands every year. Many of these small size statues were nude figures of the mother goddess and contained accurate observations of the human figure. Greek sculptors of the Archaic period were impressed by the naturalistic qualities in Cypriot sculpture and a direct result of this was that they themselves began to pay more attention to natural forms and natural proportions in their work. Another aspect of Cypriot sculpture that impressed them was the freedom Cypriot artists enjoyed in making their work, they seemed unafferected by restricting traditions and religious rules. Under the impact of Cypriot sculpture the statues of Greek gods began to appear with increasingly less clothing and eventually at the time of the sculptor Phidias all archaic rules were abandoned in favour of a more natural representation. Greek sculpture had entered its classical period. One of the most famous Greek statues of the classical period, the Aphrodite of Cnidus by Praxiteles, was inspired by a statuette of the goddess from Cyprus.

In spite of the relative freedom Cyprus enjoyed under the Persians there was a strong anti-Persian feeling on the island which culminated in revolt in 499. The strongholds of this sentiment were the towns of Salamis and Soli.

At that time Gorgos was King of Salamis. His brother Onesilus had been urging him to revolt for some time, without success, so one day when the king was out of town he shut the gates against him. King Gorgos fled to the Persians while Onesilus declared himself king and persuaded all the Cypriot cities, except Amathus, to join in a revolt against Persia.

Onesilus surrounded the pro-Persian Amathus, but before he was able to take it, a large Persian force had arrived at the gates of his own city, and this forced him to return to Salamis. The Cypriots arrayed their best troops against the invading Persians and King Onesilus volunteered personally to oppose the Persian General Artybius who commanded the enemy forces. In the ensuing battle Artybius fell but the buttle went against the Cypriots, and Onesilus was killed. The Amathusians, who had allied themselves with the Persians sent his head to be hung up over one of the gates of their city. Months later bees hived in the bleached cranium and an oracle advised the people to bury it and pay honours to Onesilus as a hero. The Amathusians obeyed the oracle and established an annual festival, which they called the Festival of the Cranium, in honour of their slain enemy.

KING EVAGORAS I OF SALAMIS

In 415BC a Tyrian adventurer named Abdemon, supported by the King of Citium, murdered the King of Salamis and seated himself on his throne. The city became a dangerous place for Greek nobles and Prince Evagoras, a descendant of the founder of the city, Teucer, took refuge in Cilicia. There, he gathered a group of about fifty followers. Four years later he returned with his little band and forcing an entrance at a postern gate he immediately attacked the palace and captured it, to the amazement of the citizens who watched the lightning battle from a safe distance.

The Great King of Persia did not seem to object to the re-establishment of the Greek dynasty in Salamis, but when Evagoras gradually increased his power at the expense of other Cypriot kings the Persians became suspicious. However, Evagoras managed to gain their confidence by continuing to pay the annual tribute and by bribing Persian officials with suitable presents. Eventually, either by force of arms or by persuasion, he brought most of Cyprus under his rule. Three Cypriot kings who resisted Evagoras, fearful of their safety, appealed to the Great King for help, alleging that Evagoras murdered King Anaxagoras, a friend of Persia. The Persian King took these allegations seriously and sent an expeditionary force at the enormous expense of 15,000 talents. The expedition failed and Evagoras took the opportunity to destroy the rest of his enemies in Cyprus.

After the failure of the Persian expedition against him, Evagoras found himself in an unassailable position. He was in alliance with Egypt,

had secret help from Athens, a fleet of ninety triremes, a personal army of six thousand and many more thousands at the command of his allies. At one time he crossed into Phoenicia and occupied a number of important coastal cities, including Tyre, and detached Cilicia from the Persian Empire. The Great King had to act and he ordered a land and sea expedition against Cyprus under the joint command of Erontes and Tiribazus. When the fighting began Evagoras achieved some important victories but at a crucial moment in the war his Egyptian allies abandoned him and he was forced to accept peace terms from his enemies. Under these terms Evagoras retained the throne of Salamis but agreed to give up the rest of Cyprus, to pay a fixed tribute and to be subject to Artaxerxes 'as king to king'. This was a good bargain for Evagoras and says much for his negotiating skills, for the Great King did not usually come to terms with his enemies until they were safely in chains and had agreed to serve him as 'a slave his master'.

And so the ten year war of Cyprus against Persia came to a sad end. It cost the city of Salamis to go bankrupt and this caused internal disturbances by the dissatisfied population. Evagoras lived six more years but his rule became increasingly unpopular. In 374BC he was murdered on the instructions of one Nicoreon who had claimed that both the King and his son were having an affair with his daughter.

ALEXANDER THE GREAT AND HIS SUCCESSORS

After the failure of the wars of Evagoras, the Persians followed a policy of oppression against the Greek Cypriots and their culture. This created resentment and hostility to say the least, among the Cypriots, who took the first opportunity to rid themselves of the Persian rule. When Alexander the Great began his campaign in Asia the Cypriots supported him enthusiastically with materials of war and men. At the seige of the Port of Tyre, which Alexander had to subdue before he was able to march further east, the Cypriots supplied him with a fleet of 120 quinqueremes, considered to be the most effective war ships of the time; (a Cypriot invention; warships with five oarsmen to each oar. Previously, ships large enough to have more than two men per oar were often in the habit of breaking apart). The Cypriots played a leading part in the capture of this strategic port, with King Pnytagoras of Salamis sharing command of the fleet with Alexander.

Many Cypriots followed Alexander to Egypt and helped him conquer the Land of the Pharaohs, then returned with him to Cyprus and were honoured with magnificent processions, sacrifices and competitions. It is recorded that the Athenian tragic actor Athenodorus took part in the drama competition and won the first prize. The Cypriots kings vied with each other to be generous to Alexander who, in his turn, gave them valuable gifts. King Pnytagoras of Salamis, whose personal flagship sunk at the battle of Tyre, and who consequently nearly lost his life, was rewarded with the copper producing town of Tamassus.

From Cyprus Alexander crossed into Syria to pursue his war against Darius and took with him many of his Cypriot followers. Some of them were appointed by Alexander as Provincial Governors of his new Empire; others went with him as far as India. A Cypriot fleet under Admiral Hiero of Soli circumnavigated the Arabian Peninusla and got as far as the Persian Gulf, which was perhaps the first time sailors from the west had travelled so far east into uncharted waters.

After the death of Alexander, Cyprus was thrown into a series of bloody grappels between would-be successors. The Cypriot kings were divided in their support for one or the other of the generals aspiring to succeed Alexander, and this led to inter-city fighting and tragedy. For instance, the royal family of Paphos, who's story is told in another chapter, were forced to commit suicide en masse, in 311BC. Eventually Ptolemy, once general to Alexander, who had established himself as King of Egypt, took control of the island and the antiquated systems of city-kingdom was abolished in favour of a system of governorship for the entire island. The post of Governor was thought to be a great honour and was given to members of the highest distinction of the Egyptian court. This system of governorship under the Ptolemies lasted for 250 years, from 294BC to 581BC.

The Ptolemies were, for the most part, ruthless in their acquisition for Egypt of Cyprus' resources. Nevertheless, in spite of this drain on the country's resources, Cyprus suffered less under the Ptolomies than during the preceding centuries when it was continually ravaged by invasions and rivalries of the native kings.

UNDER THE ROMANS

In 58BC the Roman Claudius occupied Cyprus with the assisstance of Cilician pirates and the island became part of the Roman province of Cilicia. By this time the Ptolemaic Kingdom of Egypt was coming to the end of its existence as a major power, torn by iternal strife and Roman interference in its affairs.

Early Roman exploitation of Cyprus was harsh. Cato, the first Roman Governor of Cyprus confiscated the island's treasury and sold its contents for 7,000 talents. The interest on loans was first at 48% and defaulters were subjected to severe punishment. On one occasion when the impoverished city of Salamis was unable to pay interest on a loan, its councillors were locked in their chamber until a number of them died of starvation. Later, when the philosopher Cicero became Governor, he changed the rate of interest to 12 percent. Cicero liked the Cypriots, especially the Paphians and wrote about them in complimentary terms in a letter to his friend Rufus.

In 47BC Mark Anthony gave Cyprus as a love present to Cleopatra, a very appropriate present for the Queens of Egypt claimed to personify the Goddess of Love. However, the return of Cyprus to Ptolemaic rule was short lived for the Romans reoccupied the island after the sea battle of Actium when Anthony and Cleopatra were defeated and both committed suicide.

One of the most remarkable events which took place in Cyprus in Roman times was the conversion of Sergius Paulus, the Roman Proconsul, to Christianity by St Paul. What is significant about this event is that Sergius Paulus was the first high official of the Roman Empire to embrace Christianity. This is how the New Testament describes the event:

'So they being sent forth by the Holy Ghost, departed unto Seleucia; and from thence they sailed to Cyprus. And when they were at Salamis, they preached the word of God in the synagogues of the Jews: and they had also John to their minister. And when they had gone through the isle unto Paphos, they found a certain sorcerer, a false prophet, a Jew, whose name was Bar-Jesus:

Which was with the deputy of the country, Sergius Paulus, a prudent man; Who called for Barnabas and Saul, and desired to hear the word of God.

But Elymas the sorcerer (for so is his name by interpretation) with stood them, seeking to turn away the deputy from the faith.

Then Saul, (who also is called Paul), filled with the Holy Ghost, set his eyes on him.

And said, 0 full of all subtilty and all mischief, thou child of the devil, thou enemy of all righteousness wilt thou not cease to pervert the right ways of the Lord?

And now, behold, the hand of the Lord is upon thee, and thou shalt be blind, not seeing the sun for a season. And immediately there fell on him a mist and a darkness; and he went about seeking some to lead him by the hand.

Then the deputy, when he saw what was done, believed, being astonished at the doctrine of the Lord.'

BYZANTINE PERIOD—THE ARAB RAIDS

When Constantine the Great moved the capital of the Roman Empire to Constantinople and in effect divided the empire into two, Cyprus came under the Eastern Byzantine part. By this time the island had a substantial Christian population partly because of St Paul's early missionary work and partly because of a Roman policy to transport

93

Christian miners from Palestine to Cyprus to work in the copper mines. Contantine's decision to make Christianity the official religion of the state proved popular with the Cypriot Christians who took the opportunity to avenge themselves of the long years of oppression in the hands of the pagans. Pagan temples were burnt or turned into churches and their considerable properties confiscated; followers of the old religions were persecuted and their priests humiliated and killed; the statues of the gods were defaced or destroyed and those which survived and found their way to various museums stand with their genitals missing, their mutilation symbolising the victory of Christian modesty over Greco-Roman naturalism.

During the short reign of Julian the Apostate, who succeeded Constantine, paganism was declared a legal religion once more and the pagans of Cyprus, whose numbers remained considerable, re-asserted themselves and gave the intolerant Christians some of their own medicine. A curious result of the changes in fortune of the two religions is that some places of refuge for the persecuted, like the so-called Tombs of the Kings of Paphos, have a mixture of Pagan and Christian religious symbols scratched on their walls. However, the civilised rule of Julian came to an abrupt end two years after his accession, when he was killed in battle. Paganism was proscribed once more and the Cypriots settled into a comparatively peaceful life and developed a new civilisation.

By the seventh century religious art and architecture reached a height comparable to anything the island had seen before. There were magnificent public and private buildings, basilicas, and monasteries decorated with fine frescoes, ikons, statues and elaborate mosaics. Then, at the height of maturity of this new Byzantine culture, came catastrophy in the form of a long series of Arab raids which laid waste the island and almost exterminated its population.

The Arabs, who had embraced Mohammedanism in the seventh century AD., set out to impose their religion on other people with sword and fire. As a result of their zeal all Mediterranean countries suffered massacre and destruction to some extent, but Cyprus seems to have suffered most and its suffering continues to this day (the last Turkish (Moslem) invasion of Cyprus took place on 1974 and resulted in 6,000 dead, the expulsion of 250,000 Christian Cypriots from their homes, widespread looting, pillage and rape, and the destruction of churches and Christian religious art).

Cyprus was invaded by the Arabs with monotonous regularity for two hundred years. Every time they collected loot and slaves and left without showing any interest to remain permanently. In 692 the situation became so desperate that many Cypriots, led by Archbishop John, took the advice of the Byzantine Emperor Justinian and migrated to the stores of the Hellespont. There they founded a settlement which they named Nova Justiniana after the Emperor who had given them material assistance. But the suffering of the poor Cypriots did not end with their migration from Cyprus. Just before their arrival at Justiniana they were caught in a storm and many of them drowned, others died of some terrible disease soon afterwards.

The survivors decided to return home seven years later, but in order to repopulate the island in sufficient numbers the imperial authorities searched the provinces of the empire for more Cypriots and persuaded the Saracens of Syria to allow their Cypriot captives to return home.

The Archbishops of Cyprus still carry the title 'Archbishop of Nova Justiniana and all Cyprus' in memory of the unhappy experience in exile of their ancestors.

The worst Arab raid took place in 806 in which all major towns and villages were razed to the ground, churches and monasteries were destroyed, and thousands of people were killed. Those who escaped to the mountains were pursued there and were 'picked up one by one like eggs from abandoned nests and their heads were crushed against each other'. When the invaders left they took with them 16,000 prisoners, including the Archbishop, and sold them as slaves in Syria. The auctioneer was Judge Abu el Bactara; the Archbishop fetched 2,000 dinars. After this raid the surviving Cypriots abandoned the coastal areas and moved to the comparative safety of the mountainous interior. An awful result of the Arab raids is that there are no examples of Byzantine Art and Architecture dating to this period in Cyprus, except for foundations of buildings and floor mosaics.

Cyprus was rid of the Arabs thanks to Emperor Nikephorus Phocas who defeated them soundly at sea and on land. It took them a hundred years to recover from their defeat. A memorial of their raids is the moslem sanctuary of Umm Haram, near Larnaca, which owes its existence to one of the raids. It's story is related in a manuscript kept there:

In 649 there was an invasion of Cyprus, commanded by Muawiya, Governor of Syria. Among his followers was Ubada ibn as-Samit, a Companion of the Prophet, and his wife Umm Haram, a relative of Mohammed. According to the old manuscript,

'... that bulbul of the garden of eloquence, that nightingale of the flower garden of air speech, our Prophet (may the favour and blessing of God be upon him!) honoured with a visit the fortunate house of Umm Haram ... and after he had condescended to eat food, the sainted woman searched his august and sacred head for lice, and while thus laying down his sacred head ... he fell asleep. Now when he rose up from his holy slumber with a manifestation of joy and display of delight derived during that interval from the enjoyment of divine revelations and godly visions, that revered lady questioned him as to the cause of his smile, and his perfect joy and cheerfulness. Mohammed replied thus: "From the presence of God came to me inspiration and good tidings: A company of those of my faith will... spread holy war and forays, for the exalting of the Word of God... and will conquer the Isles of the Sea and the cities of the coast thereof, and those of my people who die will enter into High Heaven among those who enter first, without trial of torment and chastisement. Thus from the presence of God inspiration and good tidings came to me".

Thus saying, he gave that holy lady good news and made her enlightened heart to rejoice. That honoured lady growing eager for such high enterprise, and anxious to take her part with the victors by sea, preferred her request, and with 'Thou art of the first...' was declared of the first of the troop that was to war at sea, and was thus... rejoiced in heart'.

Eventually the intrepid Umm Haram and her husband, together with other followers of the Prophet, set out to conquer Cyprus. The old account continues:

'And from the ports at Tripoli they collected ships and boats and embarking on them and encircling about the seas, they came to the island of Cyprus. And on landing... the holy woman, (may God be pleased with her) was set with all honour on a mule; and on arriving at the place where now her luminous tomb is seen, they were attacked by Genoese infidels, and falling from her beast she broke her pellucid neck, and yielded up her victorious soul, and in that fragrant spot was at once buried'.

The writer of this old script goes on to say that... 'there is no doubt that for those who with earnest endeavour and with full faith make the customary and acceptable visitation to the honoured tomb and revered shrine which contains her sacred body, the Giver of Blessings in unequalled wisdom satisfies all their needs. It is the perfect favour and grace of God most High and exalted that He has made the Aunt of that most glorious of created beings an intercessor for the inhabitants of this island and the visitors who earnestly appeal to her...'

Umm Haram is the seventh most sacred place of the Moslem world. All Turkish ships coming in sight of the mosque dip their flags in homage for to the Turks Umm Haram is an intercessor with Allah, and in times of drought they believe she will implore the 'Giver of all Good' to send the longed-for rain.

97

RICHARD THE LIONHEART

The last Byzantine ruler of Cyprus, Isaac Comnenus, was an adventurer who acquired the island by deceit. A nephew of the Byzantine Emperor he was for a short while Governor of Cilicia but lost his province to the Armenians who captured him and threw him into prison. Later he was bought by the Knights Templar with a view to making a profit on him. The Emperor was extremely reluctant to buy his nephew back because of a prophesy that he would lose his throne to an Isaac, but in the end he was persuaded to do so by his wife and two distinguished noblemen who agreed to stand security against Isaac's good behaviour.

After his release Isaac was given a sum of money to raise an army in Isauria before he returned to the capital which was under constant threat frcm the crusaders in the west and the moslems in the east. Having gathered an army and a navy be sailed to Cyprus and installed himself as Governor. He had no difficulty in establishing his authority for several reasons. He was a well known member of the Royal Family, he forged documents of his appointment, and the military forces at his command were stronger than any other force in Cyprus. When news of the treachery reached Constantinople, the Emperor was furious fearing an attack on the capital itself by Isaac and his rebels. He ordered the immediate execution of Isaac's guarantors by slow death, but before he was able to take any measures against Isaac himself, he was murdered. His successor sent an army and an inefficient navy, commanded by a blind Admiral to regain Cyprus, but Isaac had advance warning of their arrival and was able to defeat them with the help of his brother-in-law William, King of Sicily.

Isaac's victory went to his head. He declared himself Holy Emperor of Cyprus, ordered the clergy to appoint a Patriarch in opposition to the Patriarch in Constantinople, and demanded that every church on the island should display a golden statue of himself. Apart from these measures which made him extremely unpopular it was believed that he committed a series of crimes, among which was the murder of his wife and his only son; that he robbed the rich of their possessions; ravished the virgins of the island, and that in a rage of anger he cut off with an axe, the leg of his old tutor. In order to secure his position as Emperor he promised Saladdin that he would refuse all assistance to the Crusaders in return for which Saladdin promised not to invade Cyprus. This is how things stood when Richard the Lionheart was forced by storms to land in Cyprus during the course of the third Crusade.

On the third day of their voyage from Italy to the Holy Land, the Crusaders met with a great storm which scattered their ships. King Richard's ship took shelter in Crete while that of his fiancee Berengaria and his sister Joanna reached Cyprus. Emperor Isaac refused to allow the ladies to land and Richard arrived a few days later to find their ship lying off Limassol at the mercy of the waves. The shipwrecked sailors who were cast on the shores were thrown into prison and their personal belongings, as well as the belongings of those who drowned, were confiscated. Apart from his agreement with Saladdin, Isaac hated the Crusaders for his own reasons. A short while prior to this incident a number of renegade Franks, who had been members of the third Crusade, arrived in Cyprus and were entertained by the inhabitants of a coastal village. Before the renegades left they looted the village, made the villagers their prisoners and took them off to Laodicea where they sold them as slaves. Among the prisoners were twenty seven women. This incident became known all over Europe and scandalised Christendom, for Christians were not supposed to sell each other to the moslems. The renegade Franks gained 7,000 besants each from this enterprise.

Richard sent two of his knights to Isaac appealing to him to free the captives and return the bodies of the dead with their belongings. Isaac refused and then followed the dramatic events which changed the course of history in Cyprus.

According to a chronicler when the messengers returned empty handed, Richard ordered his men to prepare for battle and when they were ready he said to them, 'Follow me and we will take vengeance for the wrongs which this perfidious Emperor has done to God and to us in thus unjustly keeping our pilgrims in chains'. Isaac in the meantime, expecting trouble, had armed the people of Limassol with knives, sticks and such like and lined them along the shore behind barricades made of house fixtures and whatever else could be found. Isaac himself was on horse-back in full armour, at the head of an armour troop. After a long hand-to-hand battle the English managed to push the Cypriots back and eventually entered Limassol, where they were welcomed by the resident Latin merchants. The Greek population remained indifferent, but Richard ordered that nobody was to be harmed. Isaac and his men escaped into the countryside. So Limassol with its rich stores of corn, wine and oil fell into the Crusaders' hands.

Early the following morning, the Crusaders went after Isaac who had made camp five miles outside Limassol and startled him and his soldiers, who were still asleep, with their war cries. The Cypriots fled once more leaving behind their treasury, most of their arms, the imperial standard and Isaac's tent. The tent was taken to Limassol for the use of King Richard, the Royal Standard was sent as a gift to the Church of St Edmund's at Bury St. Edmunds, where it still is.

The following Sunday, Richard married Berengaria of Navarre in the chapel of St George in Limassol. After the wedding ceremony, Berengaria was crowned Queen of England by the Archbishop of Bordeaux. That same day, Isaac sent envoys to Richard to treat for peace and a meeting was arranged between the two men. The English chroniclers have recorded that Isaac promised to join the crusade to Palestine

with 100 knights, a light cavalry of 400 and 500 footmen. He also agreed to give his only daughter to Richard as hostage. If he made these promises he had no intention of keeping them, because he knew that if he left the island he would lose his Kingdom through revolt. His visit was probably designed to help him gain information about Richard's forces. In the middle of the night Isaac left Richard's camp unnoticed and made for Nicosia.

Richard was anxious to complete the conquest of Cyprus and move on to Palestine. He marched along the coast as far as Larnaca and then sailed to Famagusta, which he found undefended and captured it. Then he marched towards Nicosia and fought a battle with Isaac who came to meet him outside the city. The battle was fierce and Isaac managed to strike a blow at Richard with his mace. However, Richard won the battle and captured Nicosia where he was welcomed by the citizens. Richard fell sick in Nicosia, perhaps as a result of the blow he received, and sent Guy de Lusignan to capture Kyrenia. The town surrendered without a fight and Isaac's daughter, who was staying at Kyrenia Castle, was taken prisoner. Isaac was devastated by the news of his daughter, which shows that he had paternal feelings in spite of his reputation for hardness and cruelty. He ordered his remaining strongholds to surrender and gave himself up to Richard with the only condition being that he was not to be put in irons. Richard accepted the endition, but in contravention of the spirit of the agreement, put him in silver chains.

Isaac was taken to Acre by the Crusaders where he died two years later. His daughter was made a royal attendant to Queen Berengaria and eventually was taken to France where she had a colourful life. Richard gathered an enormous booty from Cyprus, whose population were made to pay to him half of everything they owned; he then sold the island to the Knights Templar for 100,000 gold dinars.

THE FRANKS

The Knights of the Temple could not control the Cypriots, who resented their cruel rule, and asked Richard to take Cyprus back. Richard agreed to their request and sold the island to a new buyer, Guy de Lusignan, King of Jerusalem, who lost his kingdom to Saladdin.

The Lusignan dynasty lasted for three hundred years and in some respects this period was a golden age for Cyprus. The Lusignans built magnificent Gothic cathedrals, castles and palaces, some of which still survive, they promoted the arts, commerce, agriculture and the profitable sugar industry. Cyprus became proverbial for its wealth but this prosperity was enjoyed only by the members of the Catholic ruling class who came from various parts of Europe. The native population did not benefit at all. The Latins introduced a Medieval European system of government under which the island was divided into 100 fiefs, allocated to the same number of feudal lords who owned both the land and the people living in their area.

The Greek Cypriots, now reduced to landless serfs, suffered cultural and religious persecution. From time to time they rose against their masters but every time they failed and paid the penalty with greater oppression. Their bishops were restricted to little villages, some orthodox monks were burnt alive and for a considerable length of time they were forbidden to elect a new Archbishop.

The most remarkable King of Cyprus during the Lusignan period was Peter I (1359-1369) who saw a danger in the rising power of the Turks and tried to unite the leaders of Europe against them. For this purpose he visited most European centres of power but returned home with little more than promises. Nonetheless Peter led a number of successful attacks against the Turks and on one occasion he managed to occupy Alexandria for a short while, but he could not consolidate his gains without assistance. In the meantime Cyprus in his absence was torn by internal strife, jealousies between lords and intrigue by the competing Genoese and Venetians who had established strong commercial colonies on the island.

Peter was murdered in 1369 by a group of dissatisfied nobles while he was sleeping with one of his mistresses. His genitals were cut off and paraded through the streets of Nicosia to the satisfaction of many betrayed husbands. Peter was an attractive and adventurous spirit, admired in many parts of Europe. Petrarch and Chaucer wrote about him in their works.

THE VENETIANS AND THE TURKS

The Venetians took control of Cyprus in 1489 and ruled for eighty years. Their rule was military in character, concentrating on building defences against the menacing Turks and in the process made themselves even more unpopular than the Lusignans. When the Turks came the Cypriots were divided in their loyalties. Some of them retreated to the mountains and fought the Turks in self defence, others joined the Venetian army and others fought on the side of the Turks.

It is said that during the siege of Famagusta in 1571, the Venetians had erected upon a bastion, a hideous, though effective, spinning wheel of knives, designed to slice into little pieces any man or beast that dared to venture near. The brave Turkish General Djamboulat Bey, considered it to be the most serious threat that the Venetian army possessed and decided to destroy it at all costs. Valiantly, sword held high in his hand, he rode his horse straight into the centre of the swirling machine, destroying himself, his horse, and the terrible Venetian device.

From then until the end of the siege, from which the Turks emerged as conquerors, the ghost of Djamboulat Bey, head beneath his arm, sword still raised high, stood on that bastion and waved encouragement to his grateful army. From that day on, the spot has borne the name of the martyred Turkish hero, a timeless memorial of his brave and self-less deed, called Djamboulat Bastion.

The Venetians possessed their heroes too, however, and one in particular, Marc Antonio Bragadino, their Commander-in-Chief, famous for his courage in battle and for the gallant, proud way in which he conducted himself in the face of hideous torture by his Turkish captors.

Made prisoner after the siege, the Turkish leader Mustafa Pasha, three times had him bear his kneck to the executioner's sword, and three times the executioner slowly, tantalisingly lowered his weapon whilst the Pasha taunted his captive, asking him how it was that his Christ did not come to save him. Eventually Mustafa, being incensed at the proud calm that his prisoner was showing, ordered the executioner to cut off his ears and nose. Then for ten days he was forced to carry baskets of earth to the ramparts, and to kiss the ground outside the Pasha's tent each time he passed. After this humiliation, and still carrying himself in the proud manner of the Venetian nobleman, the poor Bragadino was hoisted up and tied to the yard-arm of the Turkish flagship and exposed to the jeers of the highspirited Turks. Eventually, with Mustafa showing how merciless he was, Bragadino's misery was lengthened yet more, even in death. Led, with much pomp and trumpetry into the great square of Famagusta, he was slowly peeled from his skin, and his body sliced into pieces of meat which were then hung from the gates of the city. His skin, stuffed with straw and tied to a cow with a red umbrella attached over it in mockery, was paraded through the town. This hideous dummy was then hung from the mast of a ship and sailed around the ports of the Mediterranean Sea, until tired of his sickly game, the cruel Pasha sold it to Bragadino's sons for a great price.

The Cypriots were glad to be rid of the harsh military rule of the Venetians and, at first welcomed the Turks who re-established the Orthodox Church of Cyprus and abolished serfdom. But soon they were bitterly disappointed for the Turks considered Cyprus as an investment rather than a province of their empire. The Grand Vizier farmed out its revenues in exchange for a fixed annual payment. The Governorship of the island was auctioned and went to the highest bidder. The result was that the population was bled beyond reason by Governors whose only purpose was to make a profit; their tax collectors' excursions into the villages resembled armed raids by bandits. Eventually the population of Cyprus under the Turks was reduced through famine from 150,000 to 25,000.

LIBERTY

CYPRUS GAINS INDEPENDENCE

In 1878 the primitive and cruel rule of the Turks came to an end and they were succeeded by the British under the terms of a defence agreement between their two countries. The Cypriots welcomed the British believing that eventually they would cede Cyprus to Greece as they had done with the Ionian Islands a few years previously.

The British administration in Cyprus was unimaginative but efficient and just. They expanded education and gave the people a large measure of personal freedom, but in spite of this progress the Cypriots

106

kept campaigning for union with Greece. The British rejected this demand. In 1933 Cypriot Nationalists caused riots and disorder in several towns which culminated in the destruction of Government House in Nicosia. In retaliation the British introduced a series of oppressive measures and sent into exile most Greek Cypriot leaders including the church leadership.

In 1955 there was an armed uprising under the leadership of Archbishop Makarios and Colonel George Grivas. The British authorities introduced Emergency Regulations and appointed General Harding as Governor; a large number of troops were brought in to deal with the situation. The troops were assisted by the Turks of Cyprus and an intelligence unit whose methods of interrogation of suspects disgraced the British Army, but they failed to defeat the urban and mountain guerillas of Colonel Grivas. In 1960, under mounting international pressure, the British Government agreed to negotiate independence terms for Cyprus with Archbishop Makarios.

Cyprus was declared an independent Republic on August 16, 1960. The last British Governor, Sir Hugh Foot, a good man who had gained the affection of the Cypriot people during his short term of office, left the island and Archbishop Makarios, who had been elected President, took over. Cyprus, at last, had its own Government after two thousand years of foreign domination.

BIBLIOGRAPHY

BAKER, SIR S.	Cyprus as I saw it in 1879.
CASSON, L.	Travelling in the Ancient World. 1974
CARY, M. and HAARHOFF, T. J.	Life and Thought in the Greek and Roman world
CHAPMAN, M. O.	Accross Cyprus 1943
CLARK, K.	The Nude 1956
FERGUSON, J.	The Religions of the Roman Empire.
FRAZER, J. G.	Golden Bough (Third Edition) 1913.
HAYES, J. B.	Eothen 1844
HOMER.	The Iliad (Translated E. V. Rieu)
HILL, G.	A History of Cyprus, 1952
HADJICOSTIS, G.	Ktima and New Paphos 1970
JASTROW, M.	Aspects of Religious Belief and Practice in Babylonia and Assyria 1911
JAMES, E. O.	The Ancient Gods 1960
KESHISHIAN, K. K.	Romantic Cyprus
LINDSAY, J.	Ribaldry of Greece 1961
LINDSAY, J.	The Ancient World 1968
LUKE, H.	Cyprus 1957
MORTON, H. V.	In the Steps of St Paul 1936
OVID.	Metamorphoses
PINSENT, J.	Myths and Legends of Ancient Greece 1969
SPYRIDAKIS, C.	A Brief History of Cyprus 1964
THUBRON, C.	Journey into Cyprus 1970

.

Also available
from the Orage Press

HISTORIC CYPRUS

by Rupert Gunnis

Rupert Gunnis is one of the founding fathers of Cypriot historiography. Whilst working as an administrator in the British Colonial Government of Cyprus in the 1930s he visited every town and city on the island, recording its interesting historic buildings and sites. In this facsimile of 1936 edition of the resulting book, not only do we gain a snapshot of a Cyprus that has now long gone, but find a text that is still surprisingly useable as a guide to the material culture of Cyprus.

Available at all good bookshops and from online retailers.

ISBN: 978-0954452391

Available
from Friction Fiction

IN SEARCH OF SIXPENCE

a novel by Michael Paraskos

As an art critic he had often written that the purpose of art is to soothe
the pain of life. But his theory faces a real-life test with a death, that of
his father, the celebrated artist Stass. Overwhelmed by feelings of
anger, guilt and loss, Michael finds himself descending into a kind of
madness in which the boundaries between fact and fiction break down.
In a terrifying alternative reality, running from London to Cyprus and
back again, in which even time seems unstable, he encounters the
horrific figure of Pound, a murderous Nazi-sympathiser, determined to
get his hands on Stass's diary. There too Michael finds the protean but
beautiful femme fatale Miss Waites, and a Chandleresque companion,
Geroud. But as art and life collide in this moving book, the question
remains whether art can ever really act as a cure for pain.

Available at all good bookshops and from online retailers.

ISBN: 978-0992924782